"Chad…please…don't do this to me!"

His mouth possessed the soft contours of her lips with lingering passion.

"I can feel the desire, Bethany, the need for more. Why the persistent denial?"

"I just know it would be a mistake."

"A mistake?"

"I can't handle it…."

"Handle what? Handle the fact that there is something good waiting to happen between us? Handle the fact that you're a woman and I'm a man?"

Laura Martin lives in a small Gloucestershire village in England with her husband, two young children and a lively sheepdog! Laura has a great love of interior design and, together with her husband, has recently completed the renovation of their Victorian cottage. Her hobbies include gardening, the theater, music and reading, and she finds great pleasure and inspiration from walking daily in the beautiful countryside around her home.

A Stranger's Love
Laura Martin

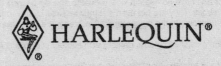

TORONTO • NEW YORK • LONDON
AMSTERDAM • PARIS • SYDNEY • HAMBURG
STOCKHOLM • ATHENS • TOKYO • MILAN • MADRID
PRAGUE • WARSAW • BUDAPEST • AUCKLAND

ISBN 0-373-17380-6

A STRANGER'S LOVE

First North American Publication 1998.

Copyright © 1995 by Laura Martin.

CHAPTER ONE

BETHANY wasn't sure exactly how long she had slept, but instinct told her it had been too long even before she opened her eyes. The rock was no longer warm now, no longer welcoming. She shifted her position a little and tried to regain the feeling of sleepy security. She was tired, far too tired to wake up. The previous night had been long and arduous—defending her chickens against the cunning fox that prowled their coop was rapidly becoming an obsession; Bethany simply couldn't afford to allow any more to escape down his greedy throat, family or no family, and she had barely got any sleep at all...

Lazily she stretched out her hand and felt a fine wetness feathering across the tanned skin of her bare arm. Immediately the first stirring of real fear prickled at her consciousness. Bethany sat up and stared, her clear green eyes wide with a mixture of amazement and horror. It surely couldn't have happened! She surely couldn't have allowed herself to be so stupid!

She had. The sea, still blue, still beautiful, was lapping hungrily around the large circular rock on all sides.

It was a secluded spot. The beach, no more than a minuscule patch of sand at this time of day, protected by craggy grey rocks that towered high above the sea, was always empty. No cars could traverse the narrow paths, few people dared to trespass across acres of fields that proclaimed immediate prosecution. It was a tiny piece of paradise and ever since Bethany had discovered it, ever since she had crossed the strip of land which belonged to the big empty house and bordered her own far more modest smallholding to negotiate the steep, difficult climb down, she had been in seventh heaven . . .

But not now. Bethany scrambled to her feet and gazed at the tartan blanket she had been lying on in disbelief, watching as the salty water encroached, soaking into its fringed woollen edges.

What on earth should she do? Bethany closed her eyes for a second in absolute despair and then opened them swiftly again. She had to think quickly. This rock, the last in a craggy chain now hidden by the swirling, heaving waters, was large but it wasn't *that* large.

She spun around wildly, her long blonde ponytail whipping at her shoulders. The sea looked dreadfully deep. Should she risk it? A ten-metre swimming badge hardly gave her the confidence to strike out in a daring bid for the shore. But what choice did she have?

Bethany wrapped the thick white towel that had been her pillow close around her skimpily clad body. 'Calm down,' she whispered to herself. 'Don't lose your head. Just calm down and think sensibly.'

She tilted her head and shouted. Over and over, her eyes glued to the cliff path up above, trying not to allow the thought that it was just hopeless, that she was simply putting off the inevitable . . .

After twenty minutes her voice had weakened and her body had become cold and weary. The evening sun had dipped low over the horizon and lost all of its warmth. Ten more tries she promised herself; after that she knew she would have to enter the sea whether she liked it or not.

And then, on the ninth call, with the salt water lapping around her ankles and the tartan rug lost for good, an apparition appeared.

She blinked several times, afraid that she was hallucinating. But no, the figure seemed real enough, more than real. Even from here she could feel the vitality, could sense the command, the presence of the man.

He had already assessed the situation. She watched with bated breath as the athletic figure traversed the cliff path with consummate ease, standing on the small strip of sand just below the craggy rock-face, legs a little apart, dark head tilted back, looking at her. Then he cupped his hands to his mouth and she heard his voice, strong and deep, heavy with a sarcasm that seemed to make a complete mockery of the terror Bethany was experiencing. 'Don't tell me—you can't swim!'

Bethany released a breath. He was no apparition. She would never have conjured up such an arrogant member of the male species to be her knight in shining armour. Besides, knights didn't wear cut-off jeans with frayed edges, or dark, dark sunglasses that were at this very moment being tossed aside on to the shingle at his feet.

'I can—just about!' Bethany's voice was barely heard, taut and strained with emotion as she watched her rescuer plunge confidently into the water and swim out with easy, efficient strokes towards the rock that was now rapidly disappearing beneath the sea.

His deeply tanned, muscular chest glistened as he heaved himself out beside her. Water streamed through his short dark hair and he smoothed it back easily from his face with one large, capable hand.

'What's your name?'

'B-Bethany. Bethany Jones.'

'Well, Bethany Jones, you're lucky I was passing,' he informed her laconically. 'This is a pretty empty spot, isn't it? I'm Chad, by the way,' he added carelessly. 'Chad Alington. How long have you been here?'

'I'm...I'm not sure.' Bethany gulped a breath, avoiding the thought that the name suited this dark, dynamic individual rather well, and glanced around at the swirling sea. 'I was very tired and I fell asleep...and the tide...well, it just seemed to come in so quickly.'

'Yeah, it has a habit of doing that,' he drawled. 'In and out, in and out, all day long.' He threw her a withering look. 'I suppose it's never occurred to you to check the times of high tide?'

'Look, it wasn't that! I knew the tide was coming in!' Bethany retorted, angry at this man's sneering tone. 'But I fell asleep—not just a light doze, a real deep... Hey! What do you think you're doing?'

He had snatched the towel from around Bethany's shoulders and tossed it away. 'Well, come on! Get in!' His voice was deep and rough with impatience. 'You're obviously cold.' His dark brown eyes surveyed her body briefly, the firm corners of his mouth curving a little in mocking amusement as Bethany instinctively wrapped her arms protectively around her suddenly far too skimpy bikini. 'I don't think we've got a great deal of time for modesty, Miss Jones,' he pointed out coolly. 'The wind's getting up and the sea is becoming choppier all the time. You do want to head back for the shore, I take it?'

'Of course I do!' Bethany snapped, confused by the arrogant brusqueness of the man. 'But I'm really not a very good swimmer——'

'Look, are you going to get in or not?' he asked impatiently. 'Because frankly I've got better things to do with my time than hang about here chatting! The sea is becoming rougher, and not only that, if we leave it much longer the path back up towards the cliff will become completely cut off.'

'But...but...I can't! It's not that easy for me!' Bethany protested frantically. 'I've just told you, I'm not much of a swimmer and the sea's so strong. I'll get caught up in the current or smashed up against the other rocks. Can't...can't you call the rescue services or something?' she added, staring hopefully into the handsome face, noticing despite everything how sensationally attractive her short-tempered, totally unsympathetic rescuer was.

'You mean you fancied a full-scale airlift? A couple of Sea King helicopters, that sort of thing?' The firm, sensuous mouth twisted derisively. 'Just because you were stupid enough to allow yourself to fall asleep? And I suppose you fancy a little bit of media coverage while you're at it?' he continued sarcastically. 'Front-page spread of the local rag? Or perhaps that isn't good enough, perhaps national coverage is more your style?'

Bethany pursed her lips and glared into the disapproving features. 'There's no need to be so unkind!' she snapped. 'You don't know how long I've been stuck here, calling and calling, waiting for somebody to come——'

'Well, I'm here now!' He interrupted bluntly, not affected in the slightest by her valiant struggle to hold back the tears. 'So you can stop getting hysterical and start listening.'

Bethany felt fierce anger rising. She couldn't believe this man! How could he be so horrible to her? Mocking her, making her feel as though she had a brain the size of a pea... 'I'm not sure I want to listen to someone as...as insensitive as you!' she replied impulsively. 'I think I'd rather drown than give your over-sized ego the satisfaction of rescuing me!'

He shrugged nonchalantly. 'Suit yourself! I'll swim back on my own.' He dived back into the water. 'See you around! Maybe.'

Bethany watched in absolute horror as he began swimming back towards the shore. 'Wait!' she yelled furiously. 'Come back! What do you think you're doing?' She glanced down at the small patch of rock at her feet and then threw a bewildered look at Chad Alington's infuriating figure. He surely wasn't going to *leave* her here—not really! No one would do that, would they? She called again, frantically this time, as the belief that maybe this man was capable of that brand of callousness took a hold. There was certainly no hesitation in his strokes, no sign that he had even heard her calling... 'I'm sorry!' Bethany yelled, as a last resort. 'I didn't mean what I said. Please... please come back!'

He took his time, circling slowly, and then, with a sigh of relief, Bethany saw that he was returning to the rock.

'That... that was a mean thing to do.' Her voice was unsteady, her eyes full of reproach.

'You said you didn't want me to rescue you,' he replied without the least sign of remorse. 'There was no way I was going to risk taking an unwilling female back to shore.' His mouth curved fluidly. 'All that struggling and screaming—very tiresome. So, are you going to get in or are we to have a little more dithering and indecisiveness first?'

You arrogant swine! Bethany thought grimly as she lowered herself into the chilly, unwelcoming brine.

'*I'll* take you back to shore,' he announced steadily. 'All you have to do is relax and rely on me. What you are not to do is start struggling like an idiot as soon as some water goes over your face, or you'll drown us both.

Got it?' Bethany bit down on her bottom lip and nodded, noting despairingly how easy it was for him to tread water—she had never, ever been able to do that properly. 'Now, lie on your back and kick with your feet a little...yes, that's fine. I'm going to put my hand under your chin like this...see? Good—just relax and stay like that.'

It was far, far easier than she had imagined. What had terrified her so much was simply not a problem now that Chad Alington had taken charge. His strong supporting hand never left her body and despite the fear and tension of the situation and the fact that she was totally, totally dependent on this arrogant disconcerting stranger, Bethany found, amazingly, that she was able to do as he had instructed and relax.

The sea had eaten up all of the beach now. After what felt like eternity, but was in fact less than five minutes, Bethany felt the delight of firm shingle beneath her feet and, with a gasp of relief, waded thankfully through the water towards the small ledge of rock which would lead them both to safety.

'Here, take my hand.' He wasn't even out of breath. Bethany glanced upwards as she felt her fingers clasped with absolute authority, and thanked heaven that, despite his foul personality, her rescuer was someone as strong and capable as this man.

Bethany, panting from the exertion of the steep climb, snatched her hand from Chad Alington's grasp as soon as they reached the top of the cliff.

She knew she should feel elated, or at the very least relieved and eternally grateful to him, now that the danger had subsided, but different emotions were taking the place of panic, fear and despair. Embarrassment and an awareness of herself in relation to this stunning

member of the opposite sex for one. She was far too
scantily clad; she had been keen to soak up as many of
the sun's rays as possible and her bikini consisted of three
floral triangles of cloth which covered little except the
bare minimum.

Bethany saw the dark eyes flick towards her body and
rest there in slow arrogant appraisal, a lazy smile trans-
forming the firm straight mouth. 'I think you need a
little adjustment,' Chad drawled with unhurried ease.

'Pardon?' She frowned, thrown into flustered confusion by the lingering gaze that made her body burn.
'What do you——?'

'The sea has rearranged your clothing for you,
Bethany,' Chad delivered conversationally. 'I'm enjoying the view, but I think maybe you would prefer it
if a little more was left to the imagination.'

Bethany felt the heated flush rise from her neck and
dropped her head, struggling clumsily to reposition her
bikini top more decently. She had climbed all the way
up the path practically topless, she thought with a pang
of despair. No wonder he had been smiling!

'I'll be all right now!' she replied stiffly, throwing him
as frosty a look as she could muster, trying to cover her
tall, slim body ineffectually with her arms.

'Where do you live?' He glanced around casually, not
in the least perturbed, it seemed, by Bethany's angry
demeanour. 'That large house is the only place for miles
around, isn't it?' He indicated the grey stone building
away towards the right. 'I understood that the beach is
a part of that property.'

'Y-Yes.' Bethany cast her eyes towards the imposing,
grey-turreted edifice. 'But I don't live there,' she
explained a trifle stiffly. 'It's empty—has been for
several years.'

'Ah, I see, so you just make use of the beach.' Dark brown eyes rested impassively on Bethany's face.

His tone was without emphasis but Bethany knew, she just *knew*, that he was trying to make a point. 'Yes,' she retorted snappily, striving without much success to keep her temper in check. 'But I don't know why you're looking at me like that! I'm not a criminal, you know! There's no crime in——'

Dark brows lifted slightly. 'Trespassing?'

'I don't do any harm,' Bethany replied tightly. 'Just——'

'Just fall asleep and get stranded on rocks in the middle of the sea!' he delivered with infuriating mockery. 'Not an everyday occurrence, I trust?'

'I've explained about that!' Bethany replied swiftly. 'There's no need to talk to me as if I'm a total idiot!'

'So it seems prosecution holds no fear for you, then?'

'What?' Bethany queried shortly. 'Look,' she continued, reading the undercurrent of mocking amusement correctly, 'I've just told you the place is empty! And anyway I don't see why I shouldn't use the beach. It's a crying shame to let such beauty go to waste, and as all I have to do is cut across a few metres of rough ground...' She halted abruptly, aware that she sounded overtly defensive. 'I don't do any harm!' she added, annoyed with herself for letting this infuriating man get under her skin.

'Of course you don't!' He was winding her up. She saw his mouth curve into a smile and refused to acknowledge the effect it had on her. 'So what happens when somebody finally buys the place?' he asked. 'Your little jaunts will have to stop then, won't they?'

'Buy the prison?' Bethany saw his brows draw down in query. 'That's what I call it,' she informed him hurriedly. 'It looks as if it was built with the sole purpose of keeping people incarcerated, don't you think? I shouldn't imagine anyone in their right mind would buy that! Even if they were mad enough to like the depressing façade, they couldn't be fool enough to take on such a crumbling wreck. It may look structurally OK from the outside, but inside it's a mess.'

She saw his interested gaze and blushed madly again.

'You know that for a fact? How?'

'Well...well, I've had a bit of a look around,' she admitted reluctantly, realising that nerves had made her gabble and consequently blurt out far too much. 'Most of the main windows are boarded up, but there's a small pantry window around the back that's open——'

'So, breaking and entering as well as trespassing!' Chad shook his head in mocking astonishment. 'You really don't have any respect for the law at all, do you, Bethany Jones!'

She blushed again, much to her own annoyance, and wondered why she was even bothering to have this conversation with so infuriating a man. 'I have to go!' she muttered stiffly, turning away. 'It's getting late.'

'Where exactly?' His voice was blunt. A strong hand had reached out.

Bethany looked down at the tanned fingers which lightly clasped her arm and then into the arrogant face. 'Would you mind letting go of me?' she retorted stiffly.

'There's no need to react as though I'm molesting you,' Chad informed her steadily. 'I just want to know where you live.'

'That's...my business!'

His gaze wandered with critical deliberation over her semi-naked body and Bethany felt the by now familiar surge of heat. 'You surely aren't going to walk back into town looking like that!'

'And what if I am?' Bethany enquired unsteadily, jerking her arm out of contact with his hand. 'I don't see that that's any concern of yours!'

'Look, lady, quit the play-acting!' Chad drawled lazily. 'You forfeited the right to act all high and mighty when you clung to that rock in the middle of the ocean and begged for rescue——'

'I did not beg!' Bethany retorted vehemently, glaring furiously at the relaxed handsome features.

'No?' He raised a dark brow and managed with that one expression to convey derisive disbelief. 'Funny. I distinctly remember a pathetic wail carrying across the water.' He threw her a challenging look. 'Wasn't that you?'

'There's no need to be sarcastic!' Bethany retorted, eyes flashing furiously.

'And there's no need for you to act like a dense child!' Chad commented smoothly. 'You know damn well that you're not exactly dressed for jaunting along the byways and highways—even rural Devon has its dangers! That outfit may be fine for the beach but it's absolutely guaranteed to give you trouble with every red-blooded male between here and town. Good God, woman! Have you looked in a mirror lately?' he asked, shaking his head disbelievingly. 'You're blonde and you're beautiful. Don't disappoint me and act like a bimbo to boot! Hardly a week passes without some report in the papers of women abducted, raped or——'

'OK! OK! I get the picture!' Bethany snapped, aware that this man's references to her physical attributes had shockingly given her a little surge of pleasure. 'I can do without the lecture, thank you very much!' She hesitated a fraction. 'I'm...I'm fully aware of how disgustingly men can behave! And despite what you so clearly would like to believe, I am not totally stupid! So there's no need for you to concern yourself. I can take care of myself perfectly well, thank you!'

'And there was I imagining I'd just rescued you from a rock in the middle of the sea!' Chad drawled with perfect and infuriating timing. 'How mistaken can a man be?'

'That was different and you know it!' Bethany blazed.

The firm mouth curved with derision. 'How?'

'Because...because...' She floundered badly, hating the fact that she felt foolish and inarticulate in front of this assured, arrogant man. 'Oh, I live over there!' she replied with breathless irritation. She raised a hand and pointed towards a simple wooden shack that nestled in a slight hollow and was almost completely hidden by a clump of sturdy oak trees. 'Well, go on then!' she added sharply, as Chad surveyed the building impassively for several silent seconds. 'Say it!'

The dark brows drew together. 'Say what, exactly?' His voice was cool, his gaze steady on Bethany's flushed face.

'"But it's a hovel!" or "You're kidding me, surely? You mean to say you actually *live* in a place like that?"' She was a good mimic and each line held a perfect imitation of the various voices that had uttered the phrases over the past eighteen months. 'Everyone thinks the same,' she informed him briskly. 'So you may as well come right out and say what you're thinking, like all the rest!'

She began striding towards her tumble-down home, regretting the loss of her well-worn and much loved sandals, that had disappeared into the sea along with the rest of her sunbathing equipment, as her soles came into contact with the rough, hard-baked earth of the mud track.

'Is it a hovel?'

'I don't think so.' He had fallen into step alongside. Bethany had hoped desperately that this far too attractive, far too controlled man would somehow just disappear and leave her in peace; she didn't want strangers upsetting her equilibrium, she didn't want this man from another world making her feel self-conscious and inadequate all over again. She had been through that once and it had not been a pleasurable experience.

Bethany threw Chad a glance that bristled animosity. 'I think it's perfectly habitable.'

'You live here permanently?'

They were through the gate now, crossing Bethany's intensively worked front garden with its neat rows of vegetables. 'Does it look like a holiday cottage?' she asked waspishly, turning to face him. 'Look, I'm damp and I'm chilly. Would you mind?'

'Would I mind what?' Chad crossed his arms across his damp, sculptured, bronzed chest and surveyed Bethany with a casual gaze.

'Leaving!' Bethany enunciated clearly, knowing full well his density was deliberate. 'If you don't mind!'

'So this is the thanks I get for saving your life, is it?' he enquired, a faint smile touching his lips. 'You're not a very grateful girl, are you?'

A *frisson* of something approaching fear scorched its way up her spine. 'What...what do you mean?' Bethany's voice was taut suddenly. It had been eighteen months since she had heard that phrase. Eighteen long months. She stiffened, unaware of what Chad was saying any more, gripping the heavy knob of the cabin door

until her knuckles whitened, remembering . . . *Grateful*!
How many times had Philip cursed her for not being
grateful? A hundred? A thousand times? She was his
wife and there were certain wifely duties that were expected. How *dared* she refuse him? How dared she cower
in the corner looking *frightened*! And after all that he
had done for her too! Didn't she have a lifestyle that a
thousand women would die for? Didn't she want for
nothing?

'P-please . . . !' There was a faint note of desperation
in Bethany's voice. Stupid, *stupid* memories! She
shouldn't be thinking about all that now. She raised her
face and implored, with wide, luminous green eyes,
'Don't . . . don't talk like that . . .'

'What's the matter?' The deep voice was sharp, but
not like Philip's; his had been higher, the vowels twisted
in that strange manner that signified someone from the
upper classes. When he had shouted her nerves had
jangled at the sound of irate instability, her body trembling because she could anticipate only too well what
would be coming next . . .

Bethany felt the firm grip of Chad's hands on her
shoulders. 'Hey! Are you with me? What is it? Don't
you feel well?'

She shook her head and tried to drag her thoughts
back from the past. This voice was strong and resonant.
It wasn't Philip. She must not think of him; that part
of her life was all gone . . . gone. He couldn't hurt her
any more . . .

Bethany inhaled a deep breath and looked up into
Chad's face. She was acting like a fool . . . The first man
to come anywhere near her since moving out here and
she was acting like a complete idiot! 'If you would
just . . . just go!' She thought she had regained control

but, to her shame, hot tears stung her eyes and with a small, strangled sob she wrenched herself from Chad's grasp, fumbled with the door-catch and flung herself inside the cabin.

'I can't leave you like this.' He moved into the clean, spartan room, practically filling the small space with his tall, broad frame, and looked at Bethany's tense face, a perplexed frown creasing his forehead. 'Was it something I said?'

Bethany shook her head and brushed the tears wildly from her cheeks with the back of her hand. It was, of course, but if she said as much, tried to explain... 'Look, please...!' She gulped back a sob and placed a trembling hand over her eyes. 'It's not you...please just go...I'll be fine...fine...' Her voice trailed away as a vision, sharp and real enough to make her frown, flew into her head. Philip with his hand raised in anger. Philip with that alcoholic leer that always, *always* made her cringe... Why was she allowing the thoughts to invade now? Why?

'You look far from fine to me!' Chad commented, surveying her huddled form with a critical eye. He moved towards her, his gaze narrowing sharply as Bethany shrank back from his outstretched hands. 'Hey, come on!' His voice was as reassuring as the hand that gently stroked the fine damp strands of hair away from Bethany's face. 'There's nothing to be afraid of! I'm not going to hurt you, for heaven's sake.' Bethany opened her mouth to speak but there were no words. She closed her eyes, her body rigid with confusion and shaky mistrust. 'Don't make me feel bad,' Chad murmured, 'I'm not always such a swine.'

'It...it doesn't matter.' Bethany pressed a clenched fist to her mouth and worked hard at preventing an embarrassing flood of tears from flowing down her cheeks.

'But it does.' Chad placed firm hands on Bethany's arms and turned her gently towards his strong, magnificent torso. 'You really must not pay any heed to my rough, brusque outer shell. My name comes from the Welsh, meaning battle—maybe that's why I come on so strong sometimes. Beneath it all I'm as weak and gentle as a kitten—honestly! Ah! That's better!' He tilted Bethany's face towards his and looked approvingly at the small half-smile that had sprung automatically to her lips. 'Does that mean I'm forgiven?' he enquired smoothly, shockingly slipping his arms around her waist, drawing her close towards the rugged physique. 'Can I leave you with my conscience absolutely clear?'

Bethany nodded, staring up into the compelling face in silence. She felt strange. She wasn't sure what was happening, but the thought of this man leaving her alone left her with an empty, hollow feeling inside.

'You...saved my life.' Bethany struggled to breathe, searching frantically through her mind for something else to say, something trivial and mundane that would break this...this ridiculous spell. 'I haven't even thanked you.'

'Don't mention it.' His voice, when it finally came, was slightly rough, husky suddenly. Dark eyes glimmered down at her, transfixing Bethany with their magnetic force. 'This is all the thanks I need...' He lowered his head and his mouth brushed hers without warning, moving slowly and surely over her parted lips in a kiss that was pure expert seduction. 'I didn't mean to make you cry,' he murmured gently, raising his head after a moment, looking down into Bethany's stunned face. 'I was angry when I rescued you from the sea. A foolish argument with someone else. I shouldn't have taken it out on you.'

'It...it doesn't matter...' Her voice was barely audible as she gazed into the stunningly handsome face. She swallowed, amazement stalling her expression. 'You...you kissed me.'

His mouth curved into an attractive smile at the sheer wonderment in Bethany's voice. 'I'm glad you noticed. Would you like me to do it again?'

It had felt good, *so* good...warm...real...

'Bethany?' Chad's voice was smooth and deep, a husky growl that sent shivers of awareness down her spine. 'If you keep looking at me like that,' he murmured warningly, 'with those desperately beautiful green eyes, that make me want to believe a million impossible things, then I may not be totally responsible for my actions. Bethany!' His voice was stronger, urgent suddenly. She felt the warmth of his breath on her face, the surge of power through his hands as they dragged her even closer against his hard, rugged length. 'Do you understand what I'm saying?' he asked sharply. One hand tilted her chin to prevent her from lowering her head. 'Are you listening, Bethany?'

She felt as if she were in a dream. Her heart was pounding, her mind barely comprehending the words that were spoken with such dynamic force. Feelings she had never experienced before were stirring inside her. The emptiness, the loneliness—they didn't seem to be there any more. How could it be? How could this man make her feel this way?

'Chad...!' His name was a scorch of emotion on her lips, no sooner spoken than crushed by the erotic pressure of his mouth.

She waited for pain, revulsion, sickness to rise up and overwhelm her, and when there was none, only passion and a deep frantic longing that leaped out of nowhere, shocking her with its intensity, Bethany sagged like a helpless invalid against the raw male strength, gripped the bronzed skin with a feverish touch that only served to heighten the electricity that sparked between them and opened her mouth wider to accept the totally dominant mouth.

'God, you're so beautiful!' She felt herself lifted after many, many minutes, her legs swung from beneath her by potent masculine arms. Chad carried her across the room to the rug that lay in front of the warming black stove, laid her gently back on to the striped rainbow rug, his mouth all the while continuing to consume her blazing skin, continuing to touch her with relentless, uncompromising passion. 'This is crazy! Absolutely crazy!' He spoke between kisses, his lips warm and moist against the soft skin of her throat, the tender places of her neck, his hands roaming and touching in a way that Bethany had never dreamed of. 'You must know what you're doing to me!'

'Y-yes.' Oh, God! What was wrong with her? She had forgotten how to breathe, how to move...

'Chad...!' Her voice was husky with tension. She couldn't even begin to understand what was going on, how or why she found herself now in this position with...with a man who oozed vitality and sexuality, and Bethany gasped in shock as she experienced the scorch of bare flesh against bare flesh, felt his hands, warm and firm, holding her close, cradling her body, moving it against his own as if it were the most precious thing in the world.

When had she *ever* been held like this? When had she ever experienced such exhilaration...such overwhelming need to be held and loved? Not until now, not until she found herself in the arms of this man, in the arms of a stranger...

She flinched. Through the heat of desire the realisation of what she was doing bit into her with all its dreadful force. What was happening to her? What was she thinking of?

'I can't!' Bethany felt Chad's body stiffen beside her, his hands cease their knowledgeable journey over her skin. She flicked open her dark lashes and found him breathing heavily, his brown eyes narrowed, scrutinising her face with an intense expression. 'No!' Bethany shook her head and closed her eyes in anguish. 'This...this *is* crazy!'

'You think I don't know that?' He raised himself up on one elbow and studied Bethany's trembling features with an unflinching gaze. 'But that doesn't mean it's wrong,' he murmured, 'does it?'

'Yes, it does!' Bethany replied wildly. 'Of course it does! It has to be!'

He reached out to touch her again, but Bethany, shamed by her own lack of self-control, afraid of the power of his touch, hit out wildly, catching the carved profile with the edge of her loosely clenched fist.

'No more!' Chad's large hand snaked out and gripped her wrist as her hand proceeded to strike out with erratic force. His dark eyes smouldered ominously. 'I think I've got the message.'

He rose fluidly, gazing at Bethany with an expression that was beyond her comprehension. She had expected fury, anger, a slap in return maybe, all the old familiar reactions, but not this control, not this smouldering tension.

She gazed into the rugged planes of Chad's face, her eyes drawn to the reddened place high up on his cheekbone where her fist had landed. 'You think I deserved this?' he enquired, gesturing to his face, a grim curve twisting his mouth as Bethany scrambled hastily to her feet.

'Y-yes!' He didn't; she knew that. But admitting as much to this man would be too humiliating for words.

'Really?' His gaze was impassive: straight and direct. She saw what he thought of her answer, what he thought of her. 'OK, if lying about it makes you feel better...' He lifted his broad shoulders in a shrug. 'I'll even apologise—then you'll really be able to salve your conscience. We can pretend that I took unfair advantage. A lie, of course, because you wanted me as much as I wanted you.'

'Don't say that!' Bethany's voice vibrated with smouldering tension. 'Get out! Get out of my house now!'

She turned then, with glistening eyes, and ran towards the doorway that led to her tiny, functional bedroom and flicked the catch firmly behind her.

I wanted him. I wanted him. The words repeated themselves endlessly in her mind. Over and over.

With trembling fingers she peeled the damp bikini from her body and rummaged like an automaton in the small chest of drawers beside her bed for something—anything—to wear. She dragged on a pair of loose jeans and buttoned up a crisp, cotton shirt.

'I *still* want him,' Bethany whispered frantically, disbelievingly. He had touched her and the ache of longing wouldn't go away.

It was a long while before she finally dragged up enough courage to open the door of her room. When she emerged, she saw that Chad Alington had gone.

CHAPTER TWO

SHE walked, trance-like, to the wooden rocking-chair by the stove and slumped down into it, closing her eyes against the memory of his touch, the feelings of desire he had so easily aroused. She couldn't bear to think about it. The taste of his mouth against her own, firm and demanding, yet with a fierce, sweet intensity...

Over and over. So many thoughts confusing her. She should be feeling ashamed, relieved that she had had the good sense to stop things before they had gone too far. Why then did she feel so...so empty, so unfulfilled...so incredibly lonely all of a sudden?

With a despairing gesture Bethany rose from the rocking-chair and, grabbing her old coat from a peg by the door, snatched up her canvas trainers and went outside.

A beautiful full moon glimmered in the night sky. Bethany, keeping her mind on the mundane, wrapped the long coat close around her slender frame and picked her way through the vegetable garden towards the small adjacent field. The goats and chickens were fine. She flicked the catch on the coop and stood up, taking in a deep breath of the fresh sea air, rubbing the back of her aching neck. It had been a long day. Maybe all she needed was a good night's sleep. Maybe everything would seem better in the morning...maybe, just maybe, she would find enough good sense to forget all about Chad Alington...

The yellow beam of light, like a beacon on the cliff-top, stopped her in her tracks. Bethany leaned her arms on the top rail of the fence and gazed towards the dark, imposing outline of the old Victorian edifice. Why hadn't she noticed it before? she wondered. Who could it be? Surely not squatters? The place was so far off the beaten track... Vandals, then?

She began to feel just a trifle uneasy. Living out here alone had been one of the hardest things to get used to, after so many months of being stifled in busy bustling cities, surrounded by people she didn't know who professed to be bosom friends, suffocated by servants, intimidated by Philip... It had taken her a good long while to get used to the emptiness, the often wild, windswept loneliness of the place, especially in winter. There had been no automatic adjustment. It had taken months before she had lain peacefully in her bed at nights, without listening out for any small sign and imagining the worst...

She opened the cabin door and picked up her air-rifle from its usual place. She wouldn't get any sleep tonight, not until she knew what was going on up there. She'd just have a quick look. The old place was a bit of an eyesore, but she had become attached to it over the months and she wouldn't want anyone doing anything really destructive to it.

Bethany stumbled and dropped her rifle on to the ground. She crouched down on all fours, her breath catching in her throat after the steep climb, and listened. Silence, just the waves crashing on the shore far below, the occasional screech of an owl. Bethany fumbled frantically on the ground for her rifle and thanked heaven, as she gripped it tightly in her hands, that the moonlight

was strong enough to see by. She craned her neck up at
the light which was coming from one of the rounded
turrets and gulped a breath. She knew her way around
inside well enough. She would be cautious, just find out
what was going on...

The stairs in this part of the building wound around
at a tight angle, and with every step Bethany took she
became more and more nervous.

Clutching her rifle, Bethany moved onwards and upwards. There was a door ahead. It wasn't properly shut.
Light, not as bright as she had first supposed, was
streaming out on to the landing, helping to guide her
way. She heard a noise, a muffled sound that sent prickles
of alarm shivering up and down her spine. This was
where he...they...whoever had chosen to hole up—
the most habitable part of the prison. I must stop calling
it that! Bethany thought desperately, inching forward so
that she could peer around the partly opened door, it
sounds so dreadful...

Her imagination had forced her into expecting any
number of desperate sights: several Mafia-types tor-
turing their prisoner, perhaps; a solitary tramp with a
bottle of methylated spirits in one hand and a knife in
the other, leaning menacingly over some poor defenceless woman; a million other equally horrendous
scenes had been conjured up by Bethany's vivid imagination—but not this, certainly *never* this.

She stared, paralysed by a shock that didn't have its
roots in horror or fear, but in a burning, indignant
mortification.

It didn't take more than a swift glance to assess what
was going on, what was *about* to go on: rugs and cushions
were strewn about the floor, a picnic hamper nestled in

the corner of the room along with a couple of kerosene lamps and several bottles of liquid refreshment.

She had known from the very first moment that this would be Chad's favourite occupation. She had sensed that uncompromising sexual quality the very first time she had set eyes on him. Why now did she feel so let down, so disheartened, such a *fool*? She should have been prepared. She should have followed her instincts and stayed in her cabin...

Bethany's gaze fixed hypnotically on the two bodies. Chad was whispering something in the woman's ear as they lay entwined together on the rugs and she was gazing up into his face and laughing happily as his strong, masculine hands travelled sensually over the sheer, clinging fabric of her dress...

Bethany, feeling like a voyeuse, turned sharply and began tiptoeing back down the staircase, desperate to get right away before she was discovered. Oh, what an idiot she would look now if he knew she was here! Gangs of men and abductors, indeed! She had been reading too many thrillers, that was her trouble!

Haste and embarrassment made her clumsy. Somehow she managed to bang the butt of the rifle on the wall. It wasn't much of a noise, just a scrape really. Bethany cursed silently and listened; clearly the seduction had reached a quiet stage. The image of the two of them stretched out on the cushions, kissing with passion and hunger, flashed unwanted into her mind. She frowned. Damn! Why on earth had she been so *stupid*?

'Who's there?'

Bethany held her breath, swivelling wide green eyes to the top of the landing. Chad appeared, his muscular frame illuminated magnificently by the light from the room, dressed in faded jeans and a denim shirt that had been dragged impatiently from the waistband of his trousers and was doing an inadequate job of hiding the broad tanned chest.

Bethany closed her eyes and pressed herself flat against the wall. There was every chance that he wouldn't see her at all; the bottom half of the winding staircase was in darkness, and unless Chad bothered to investigate further she would be all right; she would be able to escape unseen. After all, Bethany reasoned, praying desperately, he did have other, far more interesting things to attend to. The state of his clothes, clearly showed the proceedings had moved on a stage. Surely the model-type was enough to keep him occupied?

It seemed not. Chad disappeared into the room, reappeared with one of the lamps and began descending the worn stairs with a tread that was firm and intimidating in the extreme.

'Well, well! What do we have here?'

Bethany flicked open her eyes and stared speechless as the firm mouth twisted into a mocking smile. 'Bethany Jones, trespasser, no less!' Chad held the lamp high above Bethany's head and surveyed her with cool detachment. 'Just passing?' he drawled smoothly. 'Or did you come to borrow a cup of sugar?'

'Chad! Who is it, darling?'

He turned his head and shouted back up the stairs. 'Just someone I met earlier this evening, Theo, dropped by for a visit—nothing for you to worry about. Oh, no!' Chad swiftly grabbed hold of Bethany's arm to prevent her from scuttling back down the staircase. 'You don't escape that easily, my girl! I'd like to know what you're doing here—or do you consider that too presumptuous a question?'

Bethany's gaze shifted towards the landing. His dishevelled partner had appeared, her wild black hair all messed up and the buttons of her dress partly undone, allowing more than a glimpse of a frothy black lace bra.

Chad followed Bethany's gaze. 'Make yourself decent, Theo,' he drawled lazily. 'I'm bringing our visitor up.'

'You're doing no such thing!' Bethany hissed, glaring at the rugged features and trying desperately to drag her arm free from its hold. 'You can't make me enter your...your harem!'

Chad's mouth twitched for a moment and then his eyes lighted on Bethany's expression and his jaw tightened ominously. 'Just watch me!' he growled.

'Let go of my arm!' Bethany cried tightly. 'You can't do this! I'm going back home.'

'After coming all this way?' Chad enquired with mocking concern. 'In the dark too, and on such a blustery night as this? Oh, no, I couldn't allow that! Come on! Up the stairs and into my *harem*, as you inaccurately call it. As you've no doubt seen, it's a little more hospitable up there. You can take your coat off. I can even offer you a glass of wine.' His mouth curved provocatively. 'We could *really* turn it into a party—I'm perfectly willing if you are!'

'I don't want any of your kind of hospitality and I most certainly do not want a glass of wine!' Bethany snapped. She felt hot and flustered and extremely foolish, and the thought of standing before Chad and his woman trying to explain why she had walked half a mile along the cliff path in what was practically the middle of the night didn't bear thinking about.

'Don't argue with me, Bethany,' Chad replied conversationally, 'And there's no need to look quite so alarmed either. Group sex really isn't my style.' His eyes gleamed suggestively. 'I prefer more of a one to one situation, more along the lines of our experience earlier this evening.' He raised a hand and tilted her chin so that she had no choice but to look straight into his eyes. 'You know, you really should have hung in there, Bethany,' Chad advised, with a coolness that shocked her almost as much as the reference to polygamous activities. 'We could have had a pretty good time together.'

'You seemed to be having a pretty good time just a moment ago!' Bethany retorted bitterly, green eyes flashing. 'Don't let me spoil your fun!'

'I don't know quite why I'm bothering to explain,' Chad murmured, 'but I'll do it anyway. Theo's an old friend——'

'Oh, please!' Bethany released an angry breath. 'Spare me the sordid details!' She summoned up enough courage to glare at the handsome face. 'Look, I hate to disappoint you,' she continued with heavy sarcasm, 'but I have been around! It may suit you to take me for an absolute innocent, but——'

'You reacted like an innocent this afternoon. In fact you were extremely sweet,' Chad cut in smoothly, completely throwing Bethany off balance with a voice that was pure intimacy. 'Very sweet indeed—up until that moment when, for some reason, you decided that beating the life out of me was your best course of action.'

'Don't...exaggerate!' Bethany retorted unsteadily. 'And anyway, I came to my senses, that's all! Look, I'd prefer not to talk about that...particular incident! I was in shock. I'd just had a nasty experience——'

'Really?' Dark eyes gleamed down at her. Bethany felt a lurch of excitement as Chad leaned towards her. She could smell the musky scent of his aftershave, could feel the warmth of his breath on her cheek. 'I'm...I'm talking about finding myself stranded in the middle of the sea!' she retorted confusedly.

'So you're willing to admit that our experience wasn't nasty, then?' Chad enquired, watching her with amusement as she looked at him in dismay. 'That's something, I suppose. You know, Bethany, after I left your cabin I found myself wishing I'd pressed home my advantage further. Looking at you now I still can't work out why I was quite so...' He hesitated, his dark brown eyes lingering intently on Bethany's flushed face. 'So chivalrous.'

'Chivalrous!' Bethany snapped herself out of the trance-like state that Chad had so easily induced with unbelieving venom in her voice. 'What the hell would you know about being chivalrous? You...you took outrageous advantage of me! I wasn't thinking straight.... I was upset and...and——'

'Chad! What are you *doing* down there?' The plaintive wail floated down from above. Clearly Theo was becoming impatient.

'Now let me get the hell out of here!' Bethany demanded furiously, trying to drag free from his hold. 'Theo's obviously desperate for your body——'

'Oh, she has her moments,' Chad drawled, 'but then don't we all?' he added, fixing Bethany with dark, mocking eyes. 'Oh, of course, I'm sorry!' he murmured silkily. 'I forgot. You don't want me to refer to your rather passionate mistake earlier this evening, do you?'

'You...you arrogant swine!' Bethany hissed, hating the fact that he could refer to their moment together with such off-hand amusement. 'You really can't accept the fact that I didn't want you!'

'Bethany, you may be sweet but, as you've already informed me, you aren't innocent!' Chad responded with lazy provocation. 'We both know what could, what *would* have taken place between us had I elected to stay in your cabin any longer.' His eyes glinted fire, daring her to deny what they both knew to be the truth. 'Now come with me! I suddenly find that I'm not in the mood for any more of your childish bluster. If you will insist on mooching about in this highly irregular manner then you have to be prepared to face the consequences. I told you trespassing would get you into trouble——'

'Me? Trespassing? How can you stand there and say that? At least I'm not making a party of it!' Bethany cried indignantly as Chad determinedly led her up the stairs. 'I roused your interest in this place earlier this afternoon, didn't I?' she continued. 'And you decided to see what it was like for yourself——'

'What the hell is this?'

They were in the room now. Bethany glanced swiftly at Theo, who was lounging attractively on one of the cushions with an expression on her face that could have soured milk, and then looked mulishly back at Chad. 'It's a gun. What does it look like?' she snapped, snatching his hand from her arm and gripping the barrel which was at her side a little more tightly.

'And dare I ask what you thought you were doing, dressed in a coat that is at least ten sizes too big, prowling around with an air-rifle?' Chad asked irritably. 'Looking for bandits, perhaps?'

Bethany felt herself blush; a deep cerise travelled up from the base of her throat and engulfed her face swiftly and absolutely. 'I saw the light. I thought...' She hesitated.

'You thought what?' Chad's stunning eyes glinted down at her. Bethany tried to avert her gaze from the broad expanse of tanned chest revealed by his partly unbuttoned shirt and failed miserably. 'Come on, Bethany,' he chided fiercely, 'you'll have to do better than that!'

'I told you. I saw the light,' Bethany answered tightly, 'and then when I was at the bottom of the stairs I heard . . . well, I heard a noise and I thought——'

'Oh, Chad, darling! She was coming to save me!' Theo cut in with an affected little laugh. 'How very brave!'

Bethany flushed a shade deeper and threw *darling* Theo a furious look that would have turned anyone with any sense to stone. Empty-headed bimbo! she cursed silently.

'Is that right?' Chad demanded, his brows drawing together into a fierce frown. 'You weren't really creeping around here with the idea that you could save somebody with that . . . that pea-shooter!'

'Look! I saw the light from my place,' Bethany retorted. 'I wanted to make sure everything was all right. It could have been vandals. How was I to know it was you indulging in . . . in . . . ?' She struggled to put a description to the scene she had first witnessed. The vision of Chad, strong and masculine, lying on the floor with Theo flashed into her mind and wouldn't go away.

'What we were or were not doing is not the point in question and you know it!' Chad replied tersely. He placed both hands on his hips and stood directly in front of her, the denim shirt straining tautly across his shoulders, the hard expanse of tanned chest more visible than ever. 'The fact remains that you *thought* there was real danger here . . .' He shook his head in frowning disbelief. 'You're not honestly telling me you were foolish enough to imagine that you could *cope* with some sort of dangerous situation!'

'Why not?' Bethany retorted defensively. 'I had a gun!'

'You had an air-rifle,' Chad corrected. 'It's not quite the same thing! And besides, even if you were in possession of a twelve-bore, that doesn't mean you can just go around the countryside taking the law into your own hands. If you were so concerned, why didn't you phone the police?'

'Because the nearest phone is three miles away,' Bethany retorted, 'that's why!'

'You've got a truck,' Chad sighed impatiently. 'I saw it this afternoon. Wouldn't that have been a better idea?'

'Possibly,' Bethany conceded frostily, 'if it were in working order.'

'For goodness' sake!' Chad cut in savagely, his face a picture of disbelief. 'You aren't telling me that you're practically stranded out here, miles from any-where——?'

'So what if I am?' Bethany responded swiftly. 'That's no business of yours, is it? Anyway,' she continued, 'I couldn't just turn around and go back without at least trying to do *something*! Pretend I'd never seen anything? What sort of a person would that make me?'

Chad raised a dark brow and threw her a derisive look. 'A sensible one, perhaps?'

Theo tittered stupidly in the corner and Bethany turned with furious exasperation towards the door. 'That's it!' she cried. 'I didn't come here to be insulted and made a fool of! Don't let me disturb your...your *activities* a moment longer. I'll let myself out.'

'Through the pantry window, I suppose.'

Bethany turned, tight-lipped, towards Chad. 'Yes, if you must know,' she gritted. 'The same way as you so obviously got in.'

'She thinks I climbed through a grubby window in this dress!' Theo gurgled, looking down at her sleek designer label. 'Oh, Chad! The girl is priceless! Where did you find her?'

'Actually, Bethany, we used the front door,' Chad informed her evenly, ignoring the high-pitched laughter from behind. 'Perhaps you'd like to do the same.'

Bethany frowned. 'The front...? But it's locked securely. How did you...?'

'Ever heard of keys?' Theo called over, giggling. 'You know, those little metal things. They're a new invention, actually quite useful——'

'That's enough!' Chad's voice was sharp, immediately silencing Theo's sarcastic voice. 'Bethany's not an idiot.'

Oh, I am! Bethany thought desperately as the pieces of the puzzle began to fit themselves together. I am!

'You own this place?' Her voice was flat. She wondered why she hadn't thought of it before.

'Yes, that's right,' Chad replied. His mouth curled into an amused smile. The deep brown eyes glinted ominously. 'The final arrangements came through last week. You and I are neighbours now, Bethany. How do you feel about that?'

CHAPTER THREE

'I'LL accompany you back.'

'There's no need.' Bethany turned away. Her head ached with tension; the strain of keeping herself together in front of Chad was beginning to tell badly. This man was her *neighbour*? 'I'm... I'm perfectly capable of returning on my own, thank you,' she added with a half-hearted attempt at coolness.

'I'm sure you are,' Chad replied curtly. 'But it's not a particularly hospitable night; the wind has risen badly and the path back to your place is rather too near the cliff-edge for my liking. I'm taking you back to the cabin, whether you like it or not.'

'Oh, Chad, she'll be all right!' Theo interposed irritably. 'Just look at her! She's dressed for all weathers, isn't she? And she was the one who ventured out in the stupid dark anyway! What's the problem about letting her go back on her own if that's what she wants?'

'Be quiet, Theo!' Chad drawled carelessly. 'I'll drive Bethany back in the car—it won't take more than a few minutes. You can clear this place up. It's time we were getting back to the hotel anyway.'

'Getting back!' Theo rose swiftly and came over, draping her arms around Chad's neck. 'But Chad, darling, we were...' She hesitated and glanced furiously across at Bethany. 'We were having a pretty good time until she came along and ruined it. There's no need for either of us to go anywhere.'

'Look, I'm tired.' Chad kissed Theo abstractedly on the cheek and unwound her arms from his neck. 'It's been a long day and you told me yourself that you've got to get back to London early in the morning. Now just give me the keys——'

'Like hell!' Theo's shrill voice held an inordinate amount of outrage as she flounced back across the room. 'There is no way I'm staying here while——'

'Theo, don't start!' Chad cut in witheringly. 'Save your theatrical outbursts for the camera in the morning.' He held out his hand. 'Now, you are quite welcome to accompany Bethany and me back along the track to her cabin if you're afraid of being left alone here——'

'Well, how incredibly gallant of you!' Theo burst out angrily. 'You don't expect me to waste my time travelling to some shack on the side of a cliff-top do you— with her? What kind of a fool do you take me for?' Her eyes narrowed with sudden suspicion. 'You forget I know you from old, Chad Alington! It wouldn't surprise me if you've already made some kind of a move on her! She's your type, isn't she? A leggy blonde? Haven't you had more of those in your bed than any other——?'

'That's enough!' Chad's mouth tightened ominously. 'You're making a spectacle of yourself! Now, you may do as you like, Theo, stay or come with us, but either way I'm taking Bethany back home. Are you going to hand over the keys or not?'

Theo wasn't sure what to do. Bethany, disturbed by the venomous accusations, watched in embarrassed fascination as indecision crossed her carefully painted features. 'Damn you!' she gritted shakily. 'If you're so keen to waste your time on this...this country bumpkin, then do it! But it's my car—we elected to leave yours back at the hotel, remember?—and I'll be damned if I'll let

you use it to transport another of your conquests about!'
She tossed her raven-black head dramatically. 'I won't
be treated like this! I'm going back to the hotel!'

If Theo had expected some kind of emotional response, she was going to be sorely disappointed, Bethany
thought. Chad's gaze rested indifferently on Theo's face.
'OK, if that's how you want it,' he drawled, unaffected
by her scowl of animosity. He shrugged and watched
impassively as she marched over to the door in her im-
possibly high heels. 'I'll see you when I see you, Theo,'
he called as she thumped down the stairs. 'Don't drive
too fast, will you?'

'If you expect me to be in any way impressed——'
Bethany began frostily, as Chad followed her down the
staircase a moment after they had heard the predictable
screech of burning rubber on the lane outside. 'You
shouldn't let her drive, she's been drinking——'

'No, she hasn't.' Chad's voice held a hint of
amusement.

'Oh, come on!' Bethany spun around to face him, her
green eyes narrowing with dislike. 'It's not in the least
bit funny! I saw the bottles of wine. Heard what she
said. I'm not a fool, whatever you may think!'

'Meaning, I suppose,' Chad drawled, 'that you think
I plied dear, innocent Theo with drink just so I could
get my wicked way with her!'

Bethany's lips pursed grimly. 'You said it!'

'Yes, and you thought it!' Chad shot back. 'Your
opinion of me isn't particularly high, is it?'

Unconsciously her mind swung back to the cabin, the
rug, the pressure of Chad's mouth as it scorched her
lips...the scene—a prelude to lovemaking if ever there
was one—she had unwittingly stumbled upon this
evening... Oh, God! What was it about this man? she

thought angrily. Did every woman fall like an idiot at his feet? 'Can you give me one good reason why it should be?' Bethany enquired frostily. 'And don't remind me about saving my life!' she added caustically, thrusting away the treacherous thoughts. 'Because I'm honestly beginning to wonder if it wouldn't have been better if you'd left me stranded out there on the rock! I'm sure I would have been able to get back under my own steam...eventually. Anyway,' Bethany continued sharply, aware that her lie about saving herself hadn't sounded the least bit convincing, 'that's not the point! Theo's whole demeanour was that of someone who had been drinking and you let her walk out of here——'

'She hadn't touched a drop!' Chad's voice was sharp. 'Will you stop ranting on about drinking and driving, Bethany! Theo's an actress; she's got an early call in the morning. Whatever else she may do, she takes her career very seriously indeed and alcohol is a definite no-no as far as she's concerned, especially on the eve of a big job.'

Bethany frowned. She had supposed the reference to leggy blondes to be just a wild accusation made in a fit of alcoholic rage. If Theo had been sober... The picture of Chad in bed with any number of beautiful women sprang unasked for into her mind. 'But she acted as though she'd had a few...' Bethany began, thrusting away the vision, sickened by the fact that she could so nearly have joined their number.

Chad inhaled a breath and shrugged impatiently. 'Theo's always like that. It's just her way. The old seductress routine maybe, I don't know——'

'Oh, come on!' Bethany felt anger surge at his indifferent response. 'You don't expect me to believe that it was *she* who brought you here?' she delivered with dis-

believing venom. 'That *you* were the innocent party being
led astray! You upset her! You used her!' Bethany accused wildly. The need to be perverse was overwhelming
suddenly. She hated Chad Alington for causing this
emotional turbulence that seemed to have risen out of
nowhere. She had spent months and months trying to
regain her equilibrium, trying to forget about her past
life with Philip, and now here she was, here *he* was,
stirring up her well-ordered thoughts and responses.

'Your concern for Theo's welfare is extremely
touching,' Chad replied tightly. 'But, Bethany, the
woman is as hard as nails! Surely you worked that out
for yourself! She can be good fun, but she can also be
quite a bitch when she wants to be. Tonight's per-
formance is not unusual by any means, believe me!'

'Oh, isn't that just convenient!' Bethany snapped. 'She
can take care of herself, so that absolves you from all
blame! My God! You men really are all the same! You
just take what you want and never a thought for anyone
else's feelings!'

'Both Theo and I are adults, well over the age of
consent!' Chad thundered. 'We see each other from time
to time on a casual basis—an arrangement that suits her
as much as it does me.' He reached out a hand and
dragged Bethany to a halt on the bottom-most tread.
'Do you have to be so damned naïve?' His eyes flashed
to the smooth pale face in front of him. 'Theo can take
care of herself. Didn't she prove that tonight? After all,
I'm the one who's been stranded out here. So save your
sympathy—she wouldn't thank you for it!'

'Don't patronise me!' Bethany, fighting for self-
control, pulled her arm free from his hold and glared
furiously up into Chad's angular face.

'You're upset because of what Theo said, aren't you?' he murmured, with a sigh of exasperation. 'Can't you see she just used that reference to women in my bed to cause trouble?'

'I suppose you're going to tell me now that there isn't a grain of truth in it!' Bethany responded frostily. 'What was the seduction routine at my cabin this afternoon, if it wasn't just another in a long line of calculated operations? Well, come on!' she demanded shakily. 'Lie to me! After all, I'm so incredibly naïve! I'm bound to fall for any yarn you care to spin! Go on! Tell me what Theo said wasn't true!' She was shaking with emotion. This arrogant, autocratic man thought he knew it all, had already decided she was a silly little slip of a girl who had no idea about the real world...real life...

'Would there be any point?' Chad enquired bitingly. 'It seems to me that whatever I say is only going to incense you more.'

'Damned right it is!' Bethany replied instantly. 'Hell! You men are all the same——!'

'Bethany, be quiet!' His voice was deeply scathing, bored almost. 'I'm becoming sick of that clichéd phrase! You're talking absolute rubbish! Stop using this fit of temper as a shield to hide behind because you can't handle the fact that we almost made love——'

'How dare you?' She couldn't believe he was actually saying this to her. 'How dare you stand there and presume certain things that are in no way true——?'

'They're true,' Chad cut in tersely. 'You wouldn't be reacting this way if they weren't. What happened this afternoon came about because we *both* wanted it, and you know it. You're no woman of the world, Bethany, whatever you may like me to believe.' His gaze was sharp and direct. 'OK, at this particular moment you're not

being particularly sweet, but you are young and you
are——'

'Don't you *dare* call me innocent!' Bethany turned
from him, all the old familiar scenes whirring around in
her brain, making her want to be sick. Philip, in those
few short months of married life, had rid her of all innocence the very first chance he had got—how could she
ever forget that? 'How can you be so...so cruel?'

'Bethany!' Chad caught hold of her and turned her
to face him, his eyes scouring her frantic face. '*Cruel*?
What is all this, for heaven's sake? What's wrong with
you?'

'Wrong with me?' Bethany forced a choking kind of
laugh. Given half a chance, she thought, I could quite
easily become hysterical. 'Oh, nothing much! Certainly
nothing for the likes of you to worry about——'

'Bethany, I get the distinct impression that I'm missing
something here—missing something important. Care to
quit raising your voice and tell me about it?'

'Stop treating me like an idiot!' She glared up into
the handsome face, disturbed by the seemingly sincere
expression. 'You don't honestly expect me to trust
someone like you, do you?' He was confusing her and
it wasn't fair. How could he be so arrogant and blunt
one minute and full of perceptive persuasion the next?
'I don't even want you to take me back home!' She had
forced her voice to sound scathing, derisive. Better that
than weak and full of uncertainty, surely?

'Right!' He moved with lightning speed and in one
swift movement had lifted Bethany right off her feet.
'That suits me just fine!'

'What...what do you think you're doing?' she cried
shakily. 'Put me down at once! Are you listening to me?
Put me down, damn you!' Bethany struggled, but with

difficulty; her waxed coat was bulky and awkward. The air-rifle fell to the floor with a clatter as she did her best to break free from Chad's firm hold. 'You're mad!' she cried furiously, trying to push away from the solid, broad frame. 'Absolutely mad! I didn't mean I didn't want to go home at all!' she screeched. 'Stop this at once! Stop treating me like an idiot, will you?'

'Stop behaving like one, then!' They were back upstairs in an instant. Chad pushed the door open with his shoulder and re-entered the room. 'Welcome once again to my harem,' he drawled provokingly, setting her without too much finesse on to one of the large, soft floor cushions. 'Now take your coat off!'

Bethany gazed nervously up into Chad's face. 'Wh-what?'

'You heard.' He bent down beside her and began, with competent fingers, to slip the coat from Bethany's shoulders. 'How can you ever begin to feel comfortable in this thing?' His mouth curled seductively and Bethany shivered as his hands brushed lightly against the thin fabric of her shirt.

'Don't, Chad!' Her voice was faint; it took every ounce of control to keep her expression calm.

'Don't what?' He threw her an innocent look, but his tone held a hint of savage male. 'After all, isn't this what you expect of me, Bethany? Aren't I just the complete bastard? Taking what I want left, right and centre, without a thought for anyone else?'

'I'm . . . I'm not Theo!' She tried to drag her coat back over her shoulders, but met the resistance of Chad's long tanned fingers at her shoulders, was aware as their hands touched of the by now familiar lurch in the pit of her stomach. Bethany took a breath and averted her gaze from the attractive mouth that seemed to be only inches away from her own. 'She...she might have been more than happy at being brought here and seduced by you, but if you think——!'

'Me? Think?' His voice held a sarcastic edge. 'Are you sure that that's possible? After all, I am a man. All I'm capable of is using and abusing, isn't that what you've concluded? Well?' he demanded grimly, fixing her with a cold, metallic gaze. 'That's your opinion, isn't it, Bethany? We're all after one thing and one thing alone.'

'Stop it!' Bethany moistened her lips. She didn't need this. She didn't want Chad this close, delving into her thoughts and her hang-ups. So she didn't have a very good opinion of men. Could anyone blame her for that after living with Philip for so many months? She risked a glance at Chad's face. This man did, evidently. 'Will...will you please let me up?' Bethany whispered shakily. 'You're right. This afternoon...' She hesitated, desperate to form the words coherently, desperate that he should believe the truth. 'I'm...I'm not like that... What I mean is...what happened...what *nearly* happened... I'm not the sort of girl who...who——'

'But downstairs you were so keen to reject the innocent little girl image,' Chad cut in bluntly. 'What am I to believe, Bethany? How come you give off so many conflicting signals?'

She frowned, conscious of his body, strong and full of male vibrancy so close to hers. 'Do...do I?'

'You really aren't aware of it?' Chad watched her for a long moment, his eyes studying the trembling features with impassive, cold eyes. Then he took a deep breath and the grim line of his mouth softened slightly. 'You've jumped to conclusions, Bethany——' his breath was warm on her face '—about a lot of things. I'm not a sex maniac. As I told you, it's just not my style. I don't go around seducing every woman I set eyes on. Why won't you believe that what happened in your cabin wasn't an everyday occurrence? It took me as much by surprise as it did you.' He won the battle of wills, that had never been a real contest, and finally removed the coat from Bethany's body, reached for her hands, his thumbs careful and gentle as they traced a delicate circular pattern over the lightly tanned skin. 'Why won't you tell me what all this anger is really about?'

Bethany looked into the rugged face with wide nervous eyes. He was being gentle again, speaking in tones that smouldered with intensity. She wished his convincing charade didn't affect her so. He almost had her wanting to tell him about the marriage that had been a misery from foolish beginning to pathetic end, about Philip's drinking and abuse, about the humiliation and the broken dreams...

She surveyed the handsome face with an expression that bordered on the curious. Was she ready to fool herself, to *hurt* herself all over again? Hadn't she learned her lesson the hard way? Surely she wasn't so stupid as to allow herself to be tricked a second time? This sincere approach had to be a game, didn't it? Simply a different, a *clever* way of achieving the very same end.

Bethany tugged her hands free, her pulses thudding violently. 'You can't do this to me!' she cried. 'I've told you, I'm not stupid!'

'Do what?' Chad smoothed back a long silky strand of hair that had fallen over Bethany's face. 'I wasn't aware I was *doing* anything.' He took a controlled breath and considered the delicate heart-shaped face silently for a moment. 'You certainly do know how to make a man mad, Bethany,' he informed her conversationally. 'I don't even know why I'm spending this time trying to get through to you, permitting you to get under my skin like this——'

'No one's asking you to keep me here!' Bethany breathed fiercely. 'Let me up!'

'In a moment.' Chad's voice was warm, his eyes lingering intently on Bethany's face.

'You see! I was right!' Her voice was tremulous. 'You men are all the same! Stop...stop looking at me like that!' she pleaded desperately. Why did his voice, his eyes have to possess such magnetism? He was an arrogant, autocratic swine! She shouldn't be sitting here so impassively, hanging on his every word, waiting with a sharp, twisted ache of excitement to see what would happen next...

'I'm not looking at you like anything,' Chad informed her with quiet assurance. He stroked the edge of her cheek. His fingers were warm and gentle, stilling as they reached her lips, lingering seductively over the soft contours of her mouth. 'Now, why don't you calm down, have a drink, and tell me a little about yourself?'

'What?' Bethany drew a breath and tried, without much success, to put her muddled thoughts in order. 'Why?' Her brows narrowed, the deep green eyes revealing deep mistrust and suspicion. 'What do you want to know for?'

'We're neighbours, or have you forgotten?' Chad murmured softly. His fingers traced a faint pattern over her trembling chin, down along the quivering arch of her throat, managing somehow, with just the slightest of touches, to make Bethany feel as if she were losing her mind all over again. 'I feel I should know a little more about you. Why do you live in the middle of nowhere? Do you really hate people that much?'

'I don't want to talk about it.' Why didn't she get up, walk away from this man, run through the open door all the way back to her cabin? She thought about doing it, but the touch of his fingers on her skin, his look, his voice, all of it was having an incredible, crazy, hypnotic effect.

'Money is obviously very tight,' Chad observed, frowning, glancing briefly at her faded cotton shirt. 'Have you no family or friends that can help you out?'

'No.' Bethany tried not to care that she looked a mess. She fingered the frayed collar self-consciously, remembering how pleasurable it had been to rid herself of all the expensive clothes Philip had supplied her with, how much better she had felt walking from the charity shops dressed in outfits that cost only a few pounds and which had been bought with her own money. 'My reasons for living as and where I do are purely private. You may equate poverty with failure, but I don't!'

'Have I said as much?'

Bethany shifted her gaze from the sudden metallic gleam in his eyes. 'No, but I'm sure you've thought it——'

'You haven't the first idea what I think! You don't even know me!' Chad's strong tormenting hands dropped to her shoulders. Bethany could feel their latent power burning into her skin. He gave her a little shake. 'So stop putting words into my mouth. And stop looking at me as if I'm about to rape you or attack you, or even kiss you.' The superior mouth curled slightly. 'Although I can't deny the last has crossed my mind! Are you sure you wouldn't like a drink?' he continued smoothly. 'It might remove that agitated expression from your face.'

'No! I've got to get back!' Bethany scrambled clumsily to her feet and grabbed her coat from the floor with

trembling fingers, relieved that she had found the
strength and good sense from somewhere to move.

'I'm coming with you.'

He took the coat from her hands and Bethany self-
consciously allowed him to help her into it. Her gaze
fell to the floor. 'Theo's left her jacket.'

Chad glanced at it casually. 'I'll take it back some
time.'

'You're both staying at the hotel in town?' The
question had popped out before she realised. 'It looks
very nice,' she added hurriedly. 'Very... er... quaint.'

'Yes.' It sounded as if he was amused. He placed firm
hands on her arms and twisted Bethany around so that
she faced him, and she saw that he was. 'I've been there
a few days now. Theo joined me yesterday. She's an old
hand at inviting herself to places.' He calmly began to
button up her coat, as if she were little more than a child.
'I made the mistake of giving her a call and mentioning
how beautiful it was down here and the next thing I know
she's booked herself into the hotel.'

Same room? The question burned on Bethany's lips.
It took all of her self-control not to blurt it out.

Chad obviously read her mind. He slanted her a
mocking glance. 'Different rooms, if you're interested,'
he drawled with a knowing smile.

'I'm not!'

She moved away from him, but he grabbed hold of
her wrist and tugged her back. 'Hold on. I've got to
extinguish the lamps. I don't want you falling blindly
down the stairs.'

A silvery ethereal light flooded the room once the last
lamp had been put out. Bethany found her eyes drawn
mesmerically towards the impressive rugged outline, saw
the outstretched hand and had to work hard to still the

unexplainable quiver of pleasure that traversed through every part of her.

'Coming?'

She took a step forward, revelling in the firm, commanding clasp of his fingers as they curled around her own, and obediently followed Chad from the room.

Neither of them noticed the broken window immediately. Bethany removed the old heavy key from its place beneath a flowerpot and was about to insert it into the lock when Chad placed a hand on her arm.

'Just a minute.'

She watched with growing concern as he moved stealthily around the side of the cabin. When he reappeared she could see that he didn't look particularly pleased, even in the luminous half-light from the moon.

'What's the matter?'

'A window's been broken. It's all right,' he added quickly as Bethany placed a shocked hand to her mouth. 'There's no other damage. Thanks to the mesh arrangement you have over the windows, the brick didn't even go inside. Your idea?'

'What?' Bethany looked puzzled for a moment. 'Oh, the mesh? Yes. I had a local handyman make it when I first moved here. I fix it into place when I go to bed for the night. It makes me feel more secure.'

'Well, it's done a good job. Although there's been no attempt to break in. Just yobs, I should imagine, taking casual aim as they passed by.'

'Chad, what's that?' Bethany grabbed hold of the strong wrist as he turned from her. 'Oh, heavens! You're bleeding!' She turned the lower part of his arm uppermost and peered at it in the silvery moonlight. 'Look! Can you see?'

Dark brown eyes briefly surveyed the long wound. 'It's just a scratch, Bethany,' he informed her casually, 'I'll get it fixed up later. There must have been some glass sticking out of the mesh when I examined it. It's my own fault for being careless.'

'It's bleeding very badly.' Bethany turned to face him, her green eyes large with anxiety. 'Please... let me see to it for you. I'll... I'll never forgive myself if you bleed to death walking back up the track.' She hesitated and then, seeing the cold, impassive look on Chad's face, added awkwardly, 'Look, I know I've acted...' She took a deep breath and tried to work out what it was she wanted to say. 'Well, sort of crazily. Blaming you, accusing you of... all sorts of things. But I'm not usually quite so... so...'

An ebony brow lifted and suddenly there was a hint of amusement. 'Confusing?'

'Yes. No...!' Bethany shook her head and managed a wintry smile. 'Oh, I don't know what I mean. But please stay, let me see to your arm. It's the least I can do.'

It was a blessing to be out of the wind. Bethany moved silently in the darkness to the small table by the rocking-chair and lit one of the oil lamps with practised efficiency.

She had no idea why she had invited Chad into her home. No real idea of how she should behave, what she should be thinking, feeling. She had acted on impulse, driven by a surge of emotion that didn't bear close examination.

Perhaps, after eighteen months alone, she was sick of always playing safe. Maybe it was time she began to live again.

CHAPTER FOUR

'Is THAT your only source of light?'

Bethany shook off her coat and hung it on a peg by the door before answering. 'Yes, that's right.'

Chad's gaze followed Bethany around the room as she proceeded to put a match to the other strategically placed lamps. 'You don't have *any* electricity?'

'No.' She glanced across the glowing room towards Chad, who was lounging easily against the wall, and wished that her heart wouldn't leap just at the very sight of him. 'I really get along very well without it,' she continued. 'Bottled gas, oil and paraffin are very good substitutes. Adapting wasn't as difficult as you would imagine.'

'You have *had* to adapt, then?' Chad asked. 'This isn't something you've always been used to?'

'N...no.' Her reply was cautious, but she thrust her reservations aside and added with an attempt at cheerfulness, 'When my lifestyle changed, the national grid probably breathed a sigh of relief!'

Chad's mouth lifted attractively. 'You were that bad?'

'Dreadful!' Bethany admitted lightly. 'There wasn't an electrical appliance made that I didn't have in my possession.'

'So how long have you lived here?'

'Oh, just over a year and a half,' Bethany replied vaguely, seeing Chad's piercing gaze, concerned suddenly that maybe the questions might become too specific, too intrusive, too painful. She opened a drawer

in the old oak dresser that filled one end wall of the
cabin, pulled out a clean cloth and then walked over and
drew aside a curtained partition to reveal an old china
sink. 'See,' she declared with forced cheerfulness, 'I'm
not totally without conveniences!'

'Wow!' Chad sauntered over and inspected the clean,
well-worn object with mocking admiration. 'Aren't you
the lucky one? And a tap too! The miracle of clean
water.' He shook his head. 'Shame on me! And there
was I imagining you had none of the aspects of modern-
day living.' He rolled up his sleeve and thrust his arm
under the icy flow. 'The conclusions I seem to jump to
about you!'

'It probably needs stitching,' Bethany observed, with
an effort towards neutrality, as she held his arm and
cleaned the wound as gently as she could. 'I'll cut this
cloth into strips and fasten it as securely as I can but
when you get back you must go to the local hospi-
tal—— Oh!' She looked across at Chad and frowned.
'But you can't get back, can you? Theo took the car.'

'She did indeed.' He didn't, Bethany noted, seem in
the least perturbed by the fact. His mouth curved attractively. 'And your truck doesn't work, so it looks as
though I'm stranded, doesn't it?'

'So...so what are you going to do?' Bethany enquired hesitantly. 'There isn't a telephone at the...' She
had been about to say 'prison', but retrieved the of-
fending word before it left her mouth. 'At your place,'
she amended swiftly. 'And I haven't got one here...'

The broad shoulders lifted in a casual shrug. 'I'm sure
I'll think of something,' he murmured. 'It's not the end
of the world.'

Bethany hesitated. The idea of offering him a bed for
the night frightened and excited her all at the same time.

Not that she actually had anything so grand as a guest-room. Her own abode was little more than a cupboard with a bed in it... He couldn't stay here. It would be impossible.

She frowned and set her mind to the task in hand, carefully drying the long cut and wrapping around the clean, protecting cloth with hands that shook. 'There, I'm afraid that's the best I can do.' Bethany released a taut breath. Standing so close to the powerful torso, touching his tanned, hair-roughened skin, had done strange things to her equilibrium. 'Would you like a cup of coffee? Nothing fancy, of course,' she added hastily, distancing herself from the magnetic force that seemed to surround Chad Alington at all times. 'Just instant.'

'That would be nice.' A slow smile curved the sensuous mouth. 'Thank you for your work as my ministering angel, Bethany.' He glanced down at his arm, then leaned forward suddenly and kissed her mouth. 'You've done a very good job with the bandage.'

She moved nervously away to the large black stove, keeping her back to Chad, conscious of the pleasure his compliments had produced, the flush that had surged over her skin at his warm, vibrant tones, at the taste of his mouth on hers, and bustled nervously, setting the heavy kettle on to boil, fiddling with mugs and milk.

After several silent seconds of urging the hot water to boil, she murmured quietly, 'You... you could always spend the night here. I mean...' She took a huge breath and straightened some saucepans that were arranged on a shelf above the range with shaking hands. 'I haven't got a spare bed or anything ... it would just be a case of making do with the rocking-chair ... but as it's turned into such a dreadful night ... and as I——'

'OK.' Chad cut into her increasing waffle with clipped efficiency. 'But are you sure?'

'No... no.' She turned finally, after pouring hot water over the coffee in the two mugs, knowing full well that the rich brown eyes would be dancing with amusement. 'Do you take milk? It's only goats', I'm afraid. I can't think why, but the milkman declines to deliver out here.' She was waffling again. Bethany swallowed, and cursed silently at her own lack of composure.

'Black's fine.' Chad came forward and accepted the steaming brew she held out, his eyes on Bethany's face. 'You're *not* sure you want me to stay here?'

'What?' Bethany looked confused.

Chad's lips curved; he reached forward and tucked a strand of honey-coloured hair behind her ear. 'I asked you earlier if you were sure and you said no,' he murmured. 'If you're having second thoughts, then I can easily go back to——' he paused and a slight curve lifted the corners of his mouth '——the prison and camp there for the rest of the night.'

'No!' Bethany shook her head, feeling foolish beneath the magnetic gaze. 'No, it's OK.' The truth was she wanted him here. The broken window had shaken her more than she would ever admit. If Chad hadn't been around... She suddenly realised how vulnerable she was out here... all alone.

'What are you thinking about?' Chad's voice was low. 'The window?'

Bethany nodded. 'It's not very nice. Do you think they'll come back?'

'No, I shouldn't think so. And if they do, I'll be here to protect you.'

It was an immensely comforting thought. Bethany released a quiet sigh of relief. 'It really hasn't worried you at all, has it?' she asked in bewildered tones, watching Chad's relaxed features. 'How can you take it all in your stride like this?'

'Ah, that's practice, I guess,' he drawled. 'A familiarity with the dregs of human society. It's not something I care to admit to very often,' he added, seeing Bethany's puzzled expression, 'but the fact is I'm used to violence and aggression. At one time it came with the job.'

'You were a terrorist?' It was a joke, but Bethany's eyes were wide and somehow her quip came out sounding rather more serious than she had intended.

'Not quite,' Chad informed her with a lazy smile. 'I was on the other side.'

'You were in the police force?'

'No, not exactly. A special unit. Involved in high-level security. But no longer.'

'You used to be involved in…in dangerous situations?'

'It was an everyday occurrence at one time,' Chad replied smoothly, 'but not now; now I spend my days doing something far more sedentary. I write.'

'You do?' Bethany's expression showed her surprise. It was the last thing she had expected. 'What, exactly?' Her glance fell on the full and extensive bookcase on one wall of the cabin.

Chad followed her gaze. 'I doubt very much whether you'll have any of my tomes of intellect—not unless you're into biographies of obscure overseas politicians and fascist dictators.'

'Is that why you've bought that——?'

'Monstrous edifice?' Chad's mouth curled. 'Sure. The solitude attracted me the most, although I guess I must be a sucker for a hard-luck story too. From what I gather the place has never been looked after properly. The last time it was inhabited was back in the sixties. I felt it was time someone tried to do something—it's in such a beautiful location.'

'It will cost an awful lot to do the job properly,' Bethany murmured quietly.

'Is that a roundabout way of asking if I've got enough money?' Chad enquired lightly. 'There's no need to look so embarrassed. I have, as it happens,' he added, eyeing Bethany's confused expression with amusement. 'Thanks to the accumulation of some wealthy ancestors and some wise investment moves, I am perfectly able to carry out this project—don't look so worried. I won't leave the place in a worse condition than I found it.'

'You must be extremely rich,' Bethany announced stiffly.

Chad looked at her for a moment, his glance quizzical. 'Reasonably wealthy, yes.'

'A millionaire?'

Chad shrugged. 'Maybe.'

She heaved a sigh of despair. 'It changes people, do you know that? It blinds them to... to reality.'

Chad's dark brows drew together in a frown. 'Money?' He shook his head. 'You make it sound like some sort of a curse!'

'I think it is!' Bethany replied swiftly.

It was all Philip had cared about; for a while it had been all she cared about too. No, maybe she was being a little hard on herself. She had experienced no love from her husband, but money, ah, yes, plenty of that. Endless days spending mountains of cash. For a very short while it had helped to fill the void... It had been a desperately poor substitute.

'It's not so bad. Life can certainly be pretty miserable without it.' Chad's gaze shifted to the room. He strolled over to her precious collection of books. 'But then you know that, of course.' There was a pause. For a while it looked as if Chad would pursue the subject. 'So how many of these have you read?'

Bethany glanced across, breathing an inward sigh of relief, eyeing him nervously as he retrieved one or two volumes at random from the shelves. 'Every one of them,' she murmured, automatically thinking of special favourites. 'Some more than once.'

'I'm impressed.' Chad glanced at Bethany with raised brows. 'This collection's extensive. It must have taken you a long time to build up. You have quite an unusual assortment. Are you studying for a degree in English Literature by any chance?'

'No!' Bethany, annoyed by the hint of amusement in Chad's tone, swung away to retrieve some blankets from a chest in the corner of the room. She needed an excuse, some reason to place their relationship back on to its rightful footing—animosity and irritation she could handle; sympathy and seduction she could not. 'I happen to get a great deal of pleasure from reading a broad range of books, that's all! She glanced at the two volumes he held. 'I suppose you've already decided that the idea of my reading Tolstoy and Ibsen is absolutely ludicrous, but I don't see that there's any need to mock!' she retaliated, with undeserved animosity.

'Who said anything about that?' Chad replied curtly. 'Why do you always have to assume that I'm making some kind of criticism?' Dark eyes speared her face. 'It was meant as a perfectly serious question.' He drew out another volume, flicked through the pages and then slid it back. 'Living out here in absolute peace, with few distractions, seems to me to be the ideal way to acquire a degree in double-quick time; at any rate it occurred to me as a possible reason for wanting to cut yourself off from the world. Evidently,' he added tersely, pushing a well-worn copy of the works of Shakespeare back on to the shelf, 'There are other reasons.'

Bethany collected her mug and marched over to the sink, rinsing it vigorously beneath the cold running water. 'Look, I know you think it's absolutely incredible that I should live my life like this, but I do—OK?' she added, turning to face Chad with eyes that were directly defiant. 'We can't all be wealthy landowners. I'm not less of a person because I haven't got a flash car and a big house——'

'Did I say you were?' Chad enquired sharply. 'Bethany, quit the social lecture! You're winding yourself up again for no reason whatsoever. As far as I can see you're doing a remarkable job of trying to live off the land. Not many people would attempt it——'

'Don't patronise me! I don't need your nod of approval for the way I live my life!'

'Well, you sure as hell need something!' Dark eyes glittered as they met Bethany's defiant gaze. 'What's got into you all of a sudden?'

'Nothing.' Bethany's voice shook a little as she brazened it out, keeping her green eyes steady and cool on Chad's impassive features. 'I think I'll go to bed,' she murmured awkwardly. She turned and jerked open the door that led to her small cupboard-sized bedroom. 'Look, I'm sorry. The evening's affected me more than I realised and I'm feeling extremely tired...'

'Goodnight, Bethany.' He crossed the room towards her, his eyes dark, an edge of terseness in his voice. 'Let's forget the idea about my staying. Clearly you're regretting the hasty invitation you made.'

'Oh, but...!' Bethany frowned and forced herself to swallow her own foolish pride. 'Please, can't you...stay?'

'So you still prefer my presence to that of some yobs. I should be thankful for that, I suppose,' Chad remarked sardonically. 'Go and get some sleep,' he instructed. 'I'll still be here in the morning.'

The rocking-chair was empty when Bethany, hastily dressed in shorts and a T-shirt, emerged from her bedroom some seven hours later. Her first thought was that Chad had left without saying goodbye. So what if he has? she demanded silently, glancing around the neat interior of the cabin, picking up the blankets that were strewn over the back of the chair, folding them with violent, jerky movements. What difference would it make to me?

She heard the banging of metal on metal, a low, indistinct curse, and realised, with a surge of something that felt unmistakably like relief, that Chad was just outside.

Bethany peered through one of the small high windows and saw to her surprise that the bonnet of her clapped-out old truck, parked just alongside the vegetable garden, was raised and two muscular legs were revealed, lying on the ground beneath the rusty chassis.

'What on earth are you doing?' Bethany stood a few feet away, hands on slim hips, long blonde hair brushed and shining, swinging free in the early morning sunshine.

'What does it look as if I'm doing?' Chad spoke between grunts of effort. 'Hell! this damned rust! Most of these nuts feel as though they're welded on!'

'Leave it, for heaven's sake!' Bethany frowned. 'It doesn't matter.'

'Of course...it...matters!' He vented a curve as the spanner slipped.

'Look, will you stop that now!' Bethany snapped. 'I didn't ask for your help with the truck!'

She regretted her ungrateful words as soon as they were out of her mouth, as soon as Chad had slid himself out from under the vehicle and upright again. 'It doesn't work. I can fix it.' His voice was terse. He turned away and began gathering together the few rusty tools, before slamming the bonnet down with what seemed to Bethany unnecessary force.

She heaved a taut sigh and passed a hand over her aching forehead. She had lain awake for what seemed like hours, going over and over the happenings of the day, only to fall into a fitful doze as dawn broke to dream weird dreams that involved Chad and Philip in the most bizarre situations . . . situations that didn't bear thinking about in the cold light of day.

'There really was no need,' she repeated wearily, wishing she didn't feel so decidedly out of sorts. The truth was that she felt happier without the truck working. Perverse maybe, but that was the way it was. With it going she would have no excuse not to go into town, no excuse to avoid the bustling market place. She had shut herself away here for so long; with each day that passed it was becoming more and more difficult to venture out.

'Well, it's too late now,' Chad replied crisply. 'It's fixed.'

'It is?' Bethany's tone, despite her prickly mood, showed admiration and surprise. 'What was wrong with it?'

'A multitude of minor things.' Chad threw her a dismissive look and flexed his stiff shoulders.

It was going to be a very hot day later; the sun was already warm even at this early hour, and Chad had removed his denim shirt to reveal the by now familiar bronzed torso. Bethany averted her gaze and lowered her head to study her well-worn, callused hands, aware that nothing had changed; she could become as angry or as defensive as she liked, the sight of his well-muscled body still meant unexpected responses, unwanted feelings...

'When was the last time you had this thing serviced? It's a mess.'

Bethany looked up reluctantly and found her eyes straying to a streak of oil that was smeared across Chad's angled cheek. His face looked different this morning, more masculine if that were possible, more frighteningly male. Bethany observed the dark, unshaven jawline and wished he didn't look so rough and ruggedly attractive.

She shook her head, trying to think sensibly, trying not to notice another daub of oil, this time on his body, anointing the hard pectoral muscles of his chest.

'I...I don't remember. Never, I suppose,' she added, walking around to watch at a distance as Chad turned the ignition key. 'I don't use it that often,' she continued, 'only for essential supplies, and I buy most of those in bulk, so I don't have to go into town very often.'

'It's going to need new spark plugs, distributor cap, oil, any number of things,' Chad informed her briskly as the engine somewhat reluctantly fired. 'I've cleaned and realigned what's there but you're going to have to take better care of everything in the future if you want this thing to stay on the road. Not to mention getting yourself a decent selection of tools—those few I found in the back were a nightmare to work with.' He let the engine die and then jumped down from the cab. 'This thing should make it as far as town this morning. I'll write out a list of the things you'll need for the truck and you can buy them once you've dropped me off at my hotel.'

Bethany's brows drew together in query. 'The hotel?' she murmured.

Chad looked at her with narrowed eyes. 'Yes. I need to get back there this morning. You can drive me. It shouldn't take too much time out of your busy schedule,' he added with obvious sarcasm.

'Who said anything about *me* taking *you* anywhere?' Bethany enquired frostily, instantly annoyed by the commanding tones, the mocking curl of the lips.

Chad slammed the door shut and dark eyes flashed fearsomely in Bethany's direction. 'I did.'

'Well, I...I don't like being organised!' she told him stiffly, pacing backwards towards the cabin, aware of the intimidating attitude of Chad's body. 'I don't appreciate being *told* what to do. Besides,' she added, turning away from the grim expression, 'despite what you so obviously think, I have got plenty of things to do today——'

'Yes, and so have I!' Chad moved forward and placed a hand on her arm, jerking her around to face him in one smooth movement. 'Listen, girl, and listen good! It may be too much expecting a word of thanks from you for mending that damned thing, but a lift into town is the very least you can do for me!'

Bethany felt herself quail before Chad's sharp attack, aware with every part of her body just how menacing and frightening he looked right at that moment. She gulped and worked hard at appearing calm and composed, and failed miserably on both counts. 'I...I doubt that there's enough petrol,' she informed him shakily, 'and besides——'

'Besides nothing!' Chad snapped, his gleaming eyes dark with irritation. 'There's more than enough to get us the few miles into town. You can fill up for the journey back when you buy the parts you need at the garage.'

'Who said I was going to buy any parts?' Bethany replied instantly, finding from somewhere the courage, the foolish determination, not to allow this man to dictate to her.

'I did!' Chad informed her tersely. 'Remember?'

'And I don't like being organised!' Bethany snapped furiously. 'Remember that?'

He studied the flushed heart-shaped face for a couple of seconds and then suddenly she was being dragged into his arms, crushed against the oil-daubed torso. 'What is it with you, Bethany?' he demanded, and then his mouth was on hers, fierce and wild, moving with erotic intensity against the trembling softness of her lips. Bruising but not hurting, dominating but not defeating, reminding Bethany, as the seconds grew into minutes, of his power and force, of the absolute fact that he was not a man to be trifled with. She grasped the solid arms as they held her, felt the vibrancy and strength flow through her as his tongue invaded the softness of her mouth, as his hands roamed over her body, touching and exploring with erotic savagery, and felt all resistance dissolve.

She wanted to be held like this. She wanted to be kissed as if she were the only woman in the world...

When he finally lifted his head and stopped touching her, the space between them seemed to crackle and spark with electricity. Chad uttered a curse beneath his breath. 'I shouldn't have done that. I'm sorry. I lost my temper.' There was an awkward pause. 'So you are not over the moon at having the truck going again! Would you like me to disable it, just so you can carry on being stranded?'

'Don't be ridiculous!' Bethany replied sharply. 'You've...spent a lot of time on it.'

'Yes, I have.' His voice held a sarcastic edge. 'But that didn't seem to worry you before.'

Bethany marched back towards the cabin, hair swinging, her tall, slim frame rigid with pride and anger. '*You* can take the truck,' she called over her shoulder. 'Drive yourself back to your hotel. Keep it as long as you like——'

'If you're embarrassed about asking for money, don't be!' Chad cut in bluntly. 'We've already ascertained that I've got more than enough. I'll pay for what you need.'

Bethany stopped in the doorway and stared furiously into the glittering brown eyes for a second, before turning abruptly away. 'I'll get you some breakfast,' she mumbled, disconcerted by the directness of his gaze.

'You should have put me straight at the beginning,' Chad informed her curtly, 'instead of wasting time using your old trick again.'

'What do you mean?' Bethany frowned with irritation as she frantically whisked eggs into a saucepan and tried not to look as Chad made himself at home and began gathering together hot water, soap and towel from around the cabin.

'You don't even realise you're doing it, do you, half the time?' he commented, casually soaping the streaks of oil that had managed to find their way on to his arms as well as his muscular brown chest. 'That temper of yours, Bethany. You were as scratchy as hell out there and for no reason whatsoever. As you've already pointed out to me several times,' he added caustically, 'there's no shame in having very little money.'

'Look, I told you——!' Bethany began tightly, keeping her gaze fixed on the slowly cooking eggs.

'I'll give you however much you need for the parts——'

'You will not!' Bethany removed the saucepan from the stove and began slicing some thick chunks of home-made bread with a savage-looking knife. 'I don't want your charity! I don't want anyone's charity! Ever since I have lived here I have employed a philosophy that has worked extremely well—I only live within my means. If I can't afford something I don't get it. Simple as that!' She looked across to where Chad stood by the sink and was relieved to see that he had now put his shirt back on. 'I give myself a budget each week to live on and I stick to it, and at the moment that budget is all used up! Now,' she added, with a realistic attempt at a brisk in-difference that she certainly didn't feel, 'breakfast is ready. Would you like tea or coffee to drink with your eggs?'

'Accept my money!' Chad instructed angrily, as he took his seat at the small scrubbed oak table in the corner of the room. 'You can look upon it as payment for bed and breakfast or——'

'For services rendered?' Bethany finished, slapping down a pot of tea on to the table in front of him. 'Is that what you were going to say?'

'Oh, give me a break!' Chad's expression showed fierce disbelief. 'What sort of a man do you take me for?'

'A perfectly predictable one!' Bethany replied shakily. 'Don't try and fool me into believing that you don't look upon women as some sort of... of rather pleasant dis-traction, a useful pastime like all the rest——'

'What the hell are you talking about?' Chad thun-dered. 'I simply offered to pay for the parts for your truck, that's all! Now, suddenly, you've launched into your favourite man-bashing routine! The old, rather worn-out record about how we're only after one thing!'

'I don't need your charity!' Bethany yelled. Her pulses were thudding wildly, but she continued regardless. 'I've worked long and hard at finding my own independence and I won't have it ruined by someone like you!'

'Now what are you talking about?' Chad enquired harshly. 'The truck, or something else? Hell! Are you always this damned irrational in the morning?' He thrust his plate aside with a violent movement and rose from the table. 'Forget breakfast, Bethany,' he rasped. 'I suddenly find I'm not particularly hungry! Besides,' he added with a sarcastic twist of his mouth, 'I wouldn't want to accept charity, would I? How would I ever live with myself, knowing I'd taken food from someone who so obviously has to count every penny! See you around, Bethany. Enjoy your lonely, miserable existence!'

She watched him march across the room and felt herself grow cold inside. Why on earth had she been so...so...stupid? Was this what happened when you lived alone, hardly saw a soul from one month to the next? Oh, but he could hurt her so! His words like a knife, twisting in a wound that was deep and very raw from a previous existence, a previous life...

Bethany ran to the door. Chad was already halfway down the garden path. 'Where...where are you going?' she called weakly.

'Back to my hotel!'

'Please...! I didn't mean...' Bethany shook her head, furious with herself for behaving like a fool. 'Look, I meant what I said,' she continued stiffly. '*You* can take the truck.'

'Forget it!' Chad's voice was terse and sharp in the sunny morning air. He turned at the gate and she could see the lines of annoyance marking his face. 'I'll walk!'

'No!' She hesitated a fraction and added. 'No. I'm sorry... I'll take you into town.'

His gaze altered fractionally. 'And accept a loan for the parts?'

She hesitated. 'You... drive a hard bargain,' she replied breathlessly, relief washing over her as Chad retraced his steps. 'But there's no need for that. I...I think I have enough to cover what's needed.'

'I expect to be allowed to fix the window and work on the truck without having to go through all this arguing again!' he warned.

Bethany nodded sheepishly. He was railroading her and she just didn't have the means to stand up to such a forceful personality. 'If...if we're going in, I might as well get a few other things I need. Just bits and pieces,' she added, thinking about the diabolical state of her underwear, the fact that she had been desperate for several items for a long while now.

'That's more like it.' Chad slanted her a glance. 'See, Bethany,' he drawled, 'co-operation. It's not so hard when you try, is it?'

'Goodbye, then.' Bethany had pulled the truck to a halt outside the small, comfortable family-run hotel that was well placed in the middle of the market town. She turned a little self-consciously in her seat and waited for Chad to climb down from the cab.

'You make it sound as if we're never going to see each other again,' he drawled. 'How about having coffee somewhere?'

'But... but I thought...' Bethany coloured furiously as Chad lifted an ebony brow in amusement. 'I'm sure you've got plenty of things you'd rather be doing,' she murmured awkwardly.

'Nothing that can't wait for an hour or two. I've got
to make one important phone call,' Chad explained, 'but
when that's seen to, I'm free for the rest of the morning.'

'Would you help me get the parts for the truck?'
Bethany asked with childlike uncertainty. It had been
worrying her all the way into town. She hated the thought
of going into the garage on her own, having to endure
all the open, admiring glances of the young men.
'I'm . . . not too hot on things mechanical. I know you
wrote everything down for me but——'

'Stop looking petrified!' Chad opened the door and
then leant forward suddenly and dropped a kiss on to
Bethany's relieved mouth. 'Give me ten minutes. OK?'

She would have given him longer: ten minutes, ten
hours, ten days probably, but he was out right on time,
showered and changed into casual navy trousers and a
crisp white polo shirt, automatically making Bethany feel
scruffy and unkempt. 'Where do you want to go first?'

'I don't mind.'

'You said you needed some other things? Come on!
This is your opportunity to order me about. I won't bite!'

'Well . . . I suppose I should go and get some money
out of the bank,' Bethany murmured. 'How much do
you think I'll need for the parts?'

Chad calculated quickly. 'Thirty or forty pounds: a
new fan-belt, oil, plugs, distributor cap, it all adds up.
Is that too much?' he queried, glancing at Bethany's as-
tonished expression. 'Because if it is, you know
I'll——'

'No!' Bethany's reply had been sharp. 'No, I think I
can manage that,' she added quickly, smiling to soften
her reaction.

To her dismay, Chad followed her into the bank,
standing a little way off while she approached the

counter, making her feel more nervous than she already did. She wished she had had the foresight to ask him to stay outside, but now it was too late.

'Good morning, Ms Jones! How nice to see you!'

Bethany's heart sank at the sound of the bank manager's booming voice; she turned slightly to glance at Chad, but he was flicking through a couple of leaflets and was unaware of her tense expression. 'Hello, Mr...er...?'

'King, my dear. Mr King. How are you keeping? Well, I hope? Long time no see, as the saying goes. Is the postman managing to deliver all the way out to your...er...little home? I've sent quite a few letters out over the last few months inviting you to come in and see me.' The manager lowered his voice conspiratorially, but to Bethany's ears it still didn't seem low enough. 'You know, I really think it would be in your best interests to come in and have a little chat. After all, I know managing your funds can be a daunting prospect, but that's what I'm here for and there are plenty of investments and portfolios that I think would——'

'Thank you, Mr King!' Bethany interrupted anxiously. 'Thank you very much for your concern. Maybe I'll take up your offer and come in some time. But if you don't mind, I'm rather busy at the moment...' She turned and stared pointedly at Chad.

'Ah, yes! My apologies!' The bank manager beamed at Chad, who nodded curtly in return. 'I won't keep you a minute longer. Just let me know if there's anything you need.'

He backed away and Bethany heaved an inward sigh of relief. She hurriedly accepted the money the cashier handed over and stuffed the notes into her pocket.

'Did my eyes and ears deceive me or was that an understanding bank manager?' Chad enquired with a dry smile. 'Rather a rare breed nowadays for someone in your position who has to count every penny.'

'Yes...' Bethany gulped a breath and tried to steady her nerves. 'Yes, I suppose they are.'

She didn't contradict him. How could she? They were getting along so well. If she told Chad how things really were it would mean questions and more questions, and she didn't want that, not now, not ever...

The next couple of hours whizzed by and Bethany, to her surprise, found herself actually enjoying her outing in the small, bustling market town. She knew Chad Alington had a lot to do with it, of course. He was an excellent companion; calm, reassuring her with a smile when she dithered over the smallest purchase. 'I just need to get some underwear.' The admission made her blush.

Chad evidently saw the flood of cerise and smiled. 'If you like, I'll wait outside,' he offered. 'The shop looks far too small for both of us anyway.'

The boutique might have been tiny, but it held a very good selection of lingerie. Bethany's eyes were drawn to the delicate garments, the luxurious silks and satins with their feminine wisps of lace. White and cream, they looked the nicest, she decided. On impulse she reached forward and lifted a matching set of panties and bra.

'Lovely, isn't it?' The assistant had crept up on her unawares. 'It would suit your trim figure perfectly, you know! See the detail? Exclusive designs and very competitively priced, even though I say so myself. Why not treat yourself, eh?'

Bethany smiled and shook her head. 'It's gorgeous, they all are, but far, far too impractical, I'm afraid.' With a sigh she placed the hanger back on the rail, glancing out of the window to see if Chad was getting impatient.

'He'd love it, you know!' The assistant smiled and gestured towards Chad, who was walking up and down outside, head bent, hands thrust into trouser pockets. 'Go on, dear! Be a devil, take his breath away. It'll do wonders for your love-life!'

Bethany coloured at the woman's presumption. 'He's not... I mean, we're not...' Her voice trailed away. She didn't have to explain to this woman. She turned away to pick up two packets of functional cotton briefs that were displayed near the till.

'No, she'll have these.' Bethany looked up at the sound of the familiar voice, blushed a beetroot-red and averted her gaze as Chad handed over a selection of the garments she had originally been looking at. 'Right size?' He glanced at the labels and showed them in turn to Bethany, who nodded in dumbfounded silence as Chad removed the uninspiring packets from her fingers. 'My treat,' he informed her lazily, watching as the assistant determinedly took the collection of cream satin and lace and began to ring up the cost on the till before Bethany could protest. 'Don't accept any refunds,' he instructed as he handed over a wad of notes. 'This beautiful, head-strong girl is liable to say it's all a big mistake.'

He turned towards Bethany. 'And you can stop looking so angry. They're a present. I saw you looking at them.' He glanced swiftly at his watch. 'Now I'm afraid I've really got to go. I'll call for you at seven.' He bent his dark head and claimed her mouth with a slow, sure kiss that obliterated all of Bethany's questions. 'Until this evening,' he drawled. 'Oh, and promise me one thing?'

'Wh... What?' Bethany's voice was little more than a whisper as she looked up into the dark, dynamic face.

'That you'll wear something pretty to match the lingerie,' he drawled.

CHAPTER FIVE

'BETTER. Much, much better.' A smile that was pure sensation crossed the ruggedly attractive face as Chad flicked dark eyes first up and then down Bethany's freshly washed and dressed figure.

Eight hours had passed since she'd last set eyes on him, and in that time Bethany's mood had swung from annoyance and frustration to intrigue and panic and then back again, only this time her degree of irritation soared as she stood before the gleaming eyes and cursed herself for being such an idiot.

'That dress suits you.' Chad leaned back against the door-jamb and folded his arms across his broad chest. 'Quite a shock to the system, Bethany, seeing you in something that's so feminine.'

'It's just a simple sundress,' Bethany informed him coolly, fingering the light floral fabric nervously. 'I often put it on for a change—living in overalls and jeans can become rather boring.'

'So this new you had nothing whatsoever to do with my parting words, then?' Chad enquired, with a quirk of his lips. 'I can take no credit for this wonderful ugly duckling style of transformation?'

'Not at all!' Bethany threw him a dismissive smile and returned to her sewing, picking up the old jeans beside the rocking-chair and rummaging in her work-basket with as much intensity as if she were about to perform a life-saving operation instead of simply adding a patch to yet another jagged hole.

'You seem incredibly busy.' Chad crouched down bedside Bethany and stilled her searching hands with his own. 'Too busy to allow me to take you away from all this for an hour or two?'

Bethany swallowed, staring down at the large capable hand that covered her much smaller, far more fragile fingers. He smelt wonderful. Instinctively she inhaled, breathing in the glorious mixture of fresh soap and well-laundered clothes, of aftershave and pure masculinity. 'I have a lot to do.' Her voice was faint. Too faint. Bethany cursed her weakness and added in more powerful tones, 'I really need to have these jeans ready for tomorrow.'

Chad picked up the ragged denim and examined it. 'You're telling me you can't work in anything that has a hole in the knee? Come on, Bethany, you can do better than that! I half expected excuses, but nothing quite so feeble.'

'Do you mind!' Bethany flared, removing her hands from his touch, pushing back the rocking-chair so that she had space to move away. 'I don't actually remember inviting you in here! I don't actually remember accepting your invitation to... to... Oh!'

He had whipped her towards his body in one swift movement. Bethany gasped in shock as she felt her slim, fragile form pressed with uncompromising force against the hard male length, felt a weird light headiness wash over her as Chad gazed down into her upturned face with eyes that gleamed domination. 'Bethany, you know all this play-acting has got to stop,' he commanded. 'Why the games? It's a beautiful evening, very still and warm. Come on!' He took her hand, bent down to extinguish the oil lamp, and then led Bethany towards the door.

'Where...are we going?' Her voice wasn't steady, neither were her legs. Chad's uncompromising vitality and strength had taken her breath away.

'Wait and see!' He led her in silence until they were at the cliff-edge. 'Can you manage the path in those shoes—they're not what you usually wear, are they?'

Bethany glanced at Chad, her only pair of feminine shoes, the large beautiful expanse of blue sea, and then back at Chad again. 'I don't understand. Where are you taking me?' She frowned. 'The tide's in, there's no shoreline at this time of the evening.'

'We're not going right down to the shoreline. Here, take my hand,' he instructed. 'All will become clear in a moment or two.'

'It will?'

Chad smiled at Bethany's hesitant disbelief. 'Oh ye of little faith!' he quipped. 'Trust me. I do know what I'm doing.'

Bethany gasped at the sight that met her eyes once they had negotiated two-thirds of the path. She had passed the cleft in the rock numerous times, had sat on the wide, flat sheltered ledge that faced seaward often enough, but never, ever had she imagined it would be used for such a delightfully breathtaking purpose.

'How on earth did you manage this?' She turned in amazement towards Chad and smiled in wonderment. 'I can't believe it!' She gazed at the small round table, the two chairs, the candles that hardly flickered in the sultry summer air, the wine and crystal and covered dishes, and then at the beautiful scene all around: the cliffs that curved around the bay, the magnificent rocks and never-ending sea.

'A moment's inspiration,' Chad declared. 'I'm glad you like it.'

'I love it!' Bethany's eyes shone as she took her seat opposite Chad. 'However did you get it all here?'

'For the sake of basking longer under the warmth of your admiration, I'm tempted to lie and say it was the most difficult task I've ever attempted in my life,' Chad drawled humorously. 'However, I'm basically honest at heart, so I'll admit that it was just a case of carrying this small fold-up table and a couple of matching chairs down here, along with a carefully packed box which contained the cutlery and food. As you can see,' he murmured, lifting the lids from the dishes and stowing them away behind him, 'the meal's simple: cold chicken, crusty bread, salad, fruit and cheese for later, plus the necessary additions of wine and a little good cognac. Hey, that's good!' His lips curled. 'You still look impressed!'

Bethany felt her gaze drawn to the stunningly attractive face. 'How can I fail to be?' she replied simply.

The evening had a dream-like quality. Her senses were intoxicated with so many good things. She watched Chad talk over the glow of candlelight, listened to the gentle lapping of the waves, smelt the warm night air and willed the moment never to end.

'It's getting dark. We should be making a move.' Chad leaned back in his chair and gazed out at the large expanse of calm blue sea.

'It's been a lovely evening.' Bethany watched the carved profile. 'Thank you, Chad.'

'My pleasure.' He turned, leaning forward to touch her cheek with a gentle finger, his dark eyes vibrant and intense in the deepening gloom. 'Come on. It's getting cooler now.' He rose from the table and picked up one of the candles before extinguishing the rest. 'A light for you, my lady,' he announced with mock ceremony, holding out both the candle and his hand. 'I will lead the way.'

'What about our exclusive restaurant?' Bethany glanced at the table, reluctant to leave the precious spot.

'Don't worry, I'll see to it in the morning.'

The candle flickered and went out just as they reached the top of the cliff. Chad removed the glass holder from Bethany's grasp and tossed it away on to the grass.

'What...are you doing?' Bethany's query was little more than a whisper as Chad lessened the space between them.

'We don't need it.' He pulled her closer. His hands skimmed her outline, lingered briefly on the narrow waist, the slim hips and thighs. 'Do we?'

'Chad...!' Her voice quivered alarmingly in the soft summer night as his mouth slid down to cover hers with warm persuasion.

He lifted his head just a little, his mouth lingering on the sensitive lips. 'Did you wear the lingerie I bought you?' His hands fell to the buttons at the scooped neckline and with deft fingers he undid enough to reveal the delicate lacy edge of the satin bra. 'Good girl!' He drew aside the fabric of her dress a little more and bent his head to kiss the creamy mound of her breast. 'You look wonderful.' With unhurried ease he pulled down the straps from her shoulders and covered Bethany's exposed breast with one large hand, stroking carefully as he moved the strong fingers over the darkened centre.

'Chad...please...don't!' Her whispered plea came from the heart, as her body melted against the muscular frame. She felt weak, frantic, tortured by a mixture of conflicting emotions that raced through her body as he held her close, looked at her with those dark, glittering eyes. 'Don't do this to me,' she cried urgently. 'Don't spoil the evening! I can't handle it...I can't!'

She felt his body stiffen at her anguish, recognised rough incredulity in his voice. 'Handle what?' he repeated. 'Handle the fact that you're a woman and I'm a man? Handle the fact that there is something good waiting to happen between us? We only have to look at one another and the chemistry flares.' His mouth possessed the soft contours of her lips with lingering passion. 'I can feel the desire, Bethany, the need for more. Why the persistent denial? Why the pretence?'

'I just know it...it would be a mistake.'

He released her suddenly, placing her from him, his eyes scanning her frantic face with an intensity that was almost painful. 'A *mistake*?'

'Look, I...I can't explain!' Bethany wanted desperately to run, to escape that searching gaze that pierced through the gloom, but the magnetism, the animal vibrancy was too strong, far too powerful. She pulled her dress back together, every line of her body rigid with uncertainty, praying that Chad would make it easy for her. 'Things are...are complicated,' she mumbled.

'*Complicated*?' Chad's gaze narrowed suddenly. 'What's that supposed to mean?' He shook his head in disbelief. 'We've just shared a beautiful evening together... You were relaxed...lovely...' His voice trailed away as if remembering. 'How can you give off so many conflicting signals?' His voice was clipped. 'So tell me! Where's the complication? Go on!' he gritted. 'I'm making it easy for you!'

'You think this is *easy*?' Bethany took a breath and shook her head, a brief, uneven jerk that did nothing for the tense ache over her eyes, knowing with all her heart that Philip might be long since dead and buried, but that the humiliation, the lies and deceit he had forced upon her were not forgotten, were still here, affecting her, ruining her life...

'Clearly I've been misreading the situation.' Chad's voice was clipped. 'You don't wish to enlighten me——'

'I can't...!' Bethany murmured feebly. 'Please try and understand!'

'Understand? Are you kidding?' He released a taut, sharp breath. 'I don't understand you at all.' It was a statement of fact, uttered impassively. All of the desire, all of the warmth had faded from his voice. 'Goodnight, Bethany,' he murmured. 'Sorry I made such an unfortunate mistake.'

She opened her mouth to reply, but there were no words she could think of to say. Bethany hugged her arms around her body and watched the broad rugged frame disappear into the gloom. Then, reluctantly, she turned, and walked despondently back towards the cabin.

Over the next few weeks Bethany worked harder than she'd ever worked in her life before. The smallholding would have won prizes for its efficient tidiness. Not a minute passed without Bethany doing *something*. There was produce to be harvested and stored, goats to be milked, fences to be mended, clothes to be washed, even the books were brought down from their shelves and dusted methodically. Nothing escaped Bethany's industrious hands. Nothing.

And yet she still couldn't get Chad Alington out of her mind.

The building work had begun on his house, which didn't help. The constant noise, constant disruption, with lorries and diggers rumbling noisily at every hour of the day, was a continual reminder that he would one day be taking up residence.

'Perhaps I'm going mad.' Her voice was strange, disjointed in the darkness of her bedroom. She lay on her back and stared at the familiar wooden ceiling and wondered how you could tell. She hadn't felt particularly good these past few days: an unhappy combination of tiredness and nausea, with a raised temperature that made each task that much harder to complete. Not that she would allow herself to give in to it at all. Up at five every morning, in bed by nine every night. Work to a routine: that was what had got her through in the beginning when she had first bought this place, just after Philip had died; that was what would get her through again.

Bethany wiped her forehead with the back of her hand. She felt hot and sticky. She closed her eyes and tried to relax. A good night's sleep, that was what she needed . . . She had to forget all about him and relax . . .

She must have dozed off. Bethany sat up in her chaste wooden bed and cursed the raging thirst that needed to be assuaged as well as the fact that she was awake again. What time was it now? She groped for her wristwatch on the bedside table and saw with a small sigh of dejection that she had been asleep for less than an hour.

Then she heard the music: a heavy, incessant beat that thudded in the darkness. Flinging back the bedcovers, Bethany placed her feet on the small handmade rug beside the bed and padded wearily to the sink in the main room of the cabin.

He was having a party. Bethany shivered at the partly open window in her practical cotton nightdress and looked at the lights that were blazing from every window of the prison.

The scaffolding had fooled her. Evidently the builders had finished the interior. How long, Bethany wondered, since Chad had moved in? A day, a week? She had no idea. She gulped back some more water in an attempt to soothe her dry, sore throat and turned away, wrapping her arms around her body. Hell! Sleep was going to be impossible now, absolutely impossible!

Four hours later and the music was, if anything, even louder. Bethany tossed her book on to the floor and threw herself angrily out of the rumpled bed. Damn Chad Alington! she thought, searching for her canvas shoes. Did he have no consideration for others?

The party was in full swing. Bethany, shivered despite the protection of the long waxed coat wrapped securely over her nightdress, clenched her fist and hammered loudly on the heavy wooden door.

'I want to see him!' Her voice sounded croaky as she moved past the two nubile young beauties that opened the door to her. 'Where is he?'

The two women stood with their mouths agape for a few seconds, looking at the freakish figure before them, and then burst into a fit of giggles.

Bethany, ignoring the laughter that her incongruous presence produced, stormed forward across the new black and white chequered floor through the gyrating couples as she spotted Chad leaning against one of the stone pillars, his arms around an elegantly dressed female. 'Damn you!' she croaked. 'Don't you ever think of anyone except yourself?'

Reluctantly he removed his mouth from the slender neck and cast a glance in Bethany's direction, his dark eyes flicking over her mud-splattered coat, with its six-inch hem of cotton nightdress, and the canvas shoes that had long ago seen better days. 'Is something bothering you, Bethany?' he enquired drily, totally unperturbed by her sudden and unexpected appearance.

'Yes. Quite a lot, actually!' Bethany replied tightly, trying desperately not to notice that the conversation and laughter which had been all around had stilled to a quiet murmur. 'Do you know what time it is?'

He glanced at the flash of gold on the dark-haired wrist. 'A little after two.' Chad's voice was casual, his expression indifferent, but underneath the relaxed façade Bethany sensed the tangible force, the latent power that was there, always there, threatening to explode. He looked as magnificent as ever, simply dressed in black trousers and a white shirt: a stark, powerful outline amongst the glitz and glamour that surrounded him. 'But don't let that worry you, Bethany,' he continued in a provocative drawl, 'there's still plenty of chance to join in the fun.'

'Fun? What do you think you're talking about?' Bethany retorted angrily, raising her voice above the amused laughter. 'I have been trying to get to sleep for the past four hours! You think I've come all the way here to have *fun*!'

'Take it easy, Bethany!' With a sigh, he finally made the effort and extricated himself form his curvaceous companion. 'You look as if you're about to burst a blood vessel!' He tipped back his head and drained the amber-coloured liquid in his glass. 'Come on, let me get you a drink——'

'I didn't come here to socialise, damn you!' Bethany swung angrily away from his guiding arm. The guests were agog by now. Each one of the numerous pairs of eyes was fixed with rapturous attention on this mad woman who dared to make a scene and openly defy Chad.

'Bethany!' The tones were low and full of warning. 'Stop this now! You're in danger of becoming hysterical.'

'Why?' Bethany demanded wildly. 'Because I dare to spoil your precious party?' She was past caring. Her throat was burning, her head was aching, her body felt as if it were on fire. Chad had ignored her for the past four weeks and in all that time there probably hadn't been a minute of the day when he hadn't been in her thoughts. 'Just turn the music down, OK?' Bethany croaked, spinning angrily away, aware that a torrent of despairing tears was just waiting to roll down her cheeks.

'Stay right where you are!' His voice was like a gunshot. Bethany halted on her path towards the door and closed her eyes. She heard the measured footsteps behind her on the tiled floor and waited, trepidation running through every vein.

The guests waited too, evidently fascinated and enthralled by such an unexpected display of madness. Bethany saw Theo, moving in from another room with a lad who looked half her age on her arm, her features fixed in a malevolent smile, and wished the black square beneath her feet would open up and take her now, before the humiliation of the moment could become any worse.

Chad placed his hands on her shoulders and turned her very slowly, very carefully, to face him. 'You don't look well, Bethany,' he announced grimly. 'Believe me when I say what I'm about to do now will be for your own good.' And then in the next moment, before she could reply, or even think, Chad was slipping his hands around her waist and swinging her up into his arms.

'The party's over, everyone!' he announced, in tones that no sane person would dare to query. 'Thanks for coming.' He walked across the hall, with Bethany an incoherent bundle in his arms, and stuck his head around a door. 'Mike, kill the music, will you? And do me a favour,' he added, 'make sure everyone leaves.' He looked down into Bethany's stunned face. 'That will give me chance to deal with you, madam!'

'You can't do this!' Bethany's voice was as weak as her body. She knew she should be struggling like mad in his arms, fighting like a wild thing to free herself, but thinking wasn't doing—for some unexplainable reason she was without an ounce of energy.

'Don't waste your breath!' Chad instructed bluntly, taking the stairs two at a time.

'You're enjoying making a fool out of me, aren't you?' Bethany croaked miserably.

'Oh, I've not done that,' Chad replied with a dry smile, 'you've managed that particular feat all by yourself— that was quite an entrance you made this evening. You obviously aren't aware just how ridiculous you looked, storming in with that wild look on your face and an expression which threatened murder at the very least.'

'You think I care about their opinion?' Bethany retorted unsteadily, struggling against a throat that felt like fire. 'All those well-heeled city types and designer-dressed females!'

'Is there no one that meets your totally absurd criteria?' Chad enquired tersely. 'So you have grievances against all portions of society, do you?' His mouth curled derisively. 'And there was I thinking you were just a simple, straightforward man-hater!'

Bethany looked up into the uncompromising face, registered the lines of disapproval and resisted the suddenly almost overwhelming temptation to close her eyes, to sink her tired, aching body against the crisp white shirt. 'Would you mind telling me exactly where you think you're taking me?' she asked stiffly, aware with a

pang of horror that she had no idea which part of this
vast house she was now in, aware, as her eyes scanned
the newly painted walls, with their colourful tapestries
and murals, that Chad could do with her as he willed
and probably no one would be any the wiser.

'How long have you been ill?' He had traversed a long,
long corridor and had now turned a corner, flicking open
the catch of some impressive double doors with a neat
twist of his fingers. 'You're burning up, do you know
that?'

'I...I just feel a bit under the weather, that's all,'
Bethany croaked, her eyes on the vast four-poster bed
which dominated the undoubtedly masculine room.
'Look, this is ridiculous, Chad,' she continued wildly,
catching her breath in panic as he laid her carefully on
the rich gold counterpane and proceeded to strip back
the bed. 'What are you doing?'

'Now I'm warning you!' Chad informed her steadily,
catching Bethany deftly by the arm as she made a weak
attempt at escape. 'I'm in charge, and for once you are
going to do exactly as I tell you.'

'But——!'

Chad's jaw tightened, the dark eyes flashing dangerously. 'No buts! Now, sit up like a good, obedient girl
while I remove this god-awful coat, and don't say a word,
not one word!' he ordered sharply.

She wanted to cry. Chad must have seen her trembling
lower lip, for he softened his tone fractionally and
brushed the line of her jaw with his forefinger. 'You can't
go back to the cabin tonight, Bethany. I won't even consider it—you look like death warmed up. Just accept my
judgement and make the best of it. OK?' His dark glance
glittered over her flushed face for a second, and then
with a rueful shake of his head he dispensed with the

waxed coat, bending down on one knee to remove her battered canvas trainers with competent assurance. 'Now into bed,' he instructed neutrally, watching without comment as Bethany struggled self-consciously with her well-worn cotton nightdress. 'Do you feel hot or cold?' he enquired, once she had rested her head against the deliciously cool pillow.

She gulped a breath, feeling too weary to argue any longer, too ill to cry. 'Both.'

'In that case I'll go find some more blankets and then I'll bring along a couple of tablets to reduce that temperature. If it's not down by the morning I'll call a doctor out to you.'

Bethany heard the efficient click of the door and shifted her aching body in the bed. It felt wonderfully comfortable. The whole room was an impressive lesson in discreet luxury, with its rich fabrics and expensive rugs. Vast and luxurious in that understated expensive way that she knew of old. But not silk sheets, thank heaven, she thought dazedly as she sank her head deeper into the crisp linen pillow and closed her eyes, not those hated black silk sheets...

She awoke with a start some time later to find the room in total darkness. For a brief, mind-shattering moment, she imagined she was back in the old days, with Philip returning home late again, drunk and determined to wake her. She let out a small whimper of despair and immediately a soft lamp was clicked on and the unfamiliar bedroom came into dim view.

'Bethany, what is it?' She heard the strong, deep tones, saw Chad sitting beside the bed in a huge upholstered chair and found herself breathing a sigh of relief. 'Are you feeling bad?'

She nodded, closing her eyes at the pain of swallowing. 'My throat,' she whispered hoarsely, 'it hurts.'

'Let me see.' He rose from the chair and sat on the edge of the bed, swivelling the brass reading-lamp from beside the bed so that it would shed its light in the right place. 'Open wide,' Chad instructed with a small smile, 'I'm going to play doctor.' He looked at the inflamed throat for a couple of seconds and then placed a large cool hand over Bethany's burning forehead. 'Tonsillitis, by the looks of things,' he murmured. 'Your throat doesn't look very good at all. Do you want some of this water?' He helped raise Bethany up a little, supporting her back while she accepted a welcome mouthful of the iced liquid. 'Now I'm calling the doctor,' he announced. 'These paracetamol aren't going to do a lot. You need penicillin to get that throat back to normal.'

'But... but it's the middle of night!' Bethany croaked, sinking back against the pillow, watching anxiously as Chad picked up the phone beside the bed and punched in some digits. 'Far... too late.'

'What's that got to do with anything?' he enquired with a slight frown. 'You're ill and you're suffering. The sooner you get some medication inside you the better.'

She closed her eyes, unable to argue, not *wanting* to argue. It was a wonderful feeling this, she realised, to have someone else taking charge, someone else concerned enough to make the decisions. Bethany thought of her small narrow bed back at the cabin, imagined herself alone, having to cope as best she could with no phone and no way of getting to a doctor, and gave heartfelt thanks in that brief moment that Chad Alington was the dominating, arrogant swine that he was.

The doctor, a cheerful young man, new to the local practice and totally unperturbed by his fifth call of the night, arrived in due course and checked Bethany over with brisk efficiency, immediately dispensing the required penicillin and instructing her to stay in bed for the next few days or so.

Chad strolled back into the bedroom after seeing the doctor out and resumed his position by the bed.

'I'll be all right now,' Bethany murmured, watching the dark, dynamic figure as it settled itself into the chair. 'The doctor gave me some penicillin and——' Bethany swallowed and winced painfully '—and two tablets to help me get a good night's sleep. He said——'

'I know what he said,' Chad interrupted shortly. 'He repeated the fact that you're suffering from exhaustion, just as he was leaving.'

'Exhaustion?' Bethany frowned, struggling to keep her eyes open, aware that Chad didn't look particularly pleased, but not quite understanding, through the fog of illness, why. 'He . . . he didn't mention that to me, just something about having a rest, taking life easier—as if I'm capable of doing anything else just at the moment,' she added croakily, with an attempt at lightness.

'He was talking in the long term, Bethany,' Chad replied grimly, 'not just about the next couple of days! You've been overdoing it, haven't you? The doctor said you're underweight!' Chad released an exasperated breath and glared at her. 'I can picture it exactly. Up at dawn, working non-stop till you can barely see what you're doing any longer, into bed, up again the next morning. The same damnable routine, over and over! What on earth for?' he demanded irritably, his dark brows snapping together in query. 'Do you want to make yourself really ill, is that it?'

'No!' Bethany turned her head away from the fierce expression and buried her face into the pillow. 'No, I don't!'

'Well, what then?'

She couldn't reply. Chad's wrath, on top of everything else, was too much to cope with just now. She felt the flood of tears that had been held back for so long stream down her face and, with a cry of frustration, she sobbed uncontrollably into the pillow.

'Bethany, I'm sorry.' Chad released a breath of exasperation—at himself or her, Bethany couldn't tell. She felt his hands, firm and powerful on her shoulders, scorching her already heated skin, attempting to comfort, but only managing somehow to make Bethany feel a hundred times worse. 'I didn't mean to become angry, or to make you upset,' he informed her wearily.

'Well, you've...succeeded!' Bethany sobbed incoherently into the damp pillow.

'Yes, I realise that. Look, don't cry,' Chad continued softly. 'You'll just make yourself feel worse.' He stroked the silky blonde tresses back from Bethany's face and smoothed her damp cheek with the palm of his hand. 'I can be an insensitive bastard at times,' he murmured, turning her gently around to face him. 'Forget what I said, and the way that I said it. Forget everything,' Chad commanded in deep tones. 'Just take a deep breath and close your eyes.'

She gulped, winced with pain, and screwed her eyes shut tight, hardly daring to acknowledge that Chad was capable of sounding so wonderfully compassionate.

In the next moment she felt the delicious freshness of a cool cloth wiped across her flushed face and, after many silent minutes, found her mind blanking out with exhaustion, her body relaxing as she fell into a deep and most welcome sleep.

When she surfaced next it was to find Chad laid full-stretch on the bed beside her.

After the moment of complete shock had subsided to a containable level and Bethany had remembered how to breathe again, she lay on her side and looked from beneath lowered lashes at the taut dark features and tenacious jawline, watching the rhythmic breathing, noting the way certain lines around the firm hard mouth were softened in repose.

Unconsciously, she found her gaze sliding down, surveying the superb bronzed body that was only partly hidden beneath a carelessly thrown blanket, and then quickly up again with a jerk of shock, as Chad rolled in his sleep towards her and effectively lessened the space between them to only a couple of inches.

She stiffened, held her breath and waited. Nothing. He wasn't going to wake up.

Cautiously Bethany relaxed her body again and resumed her observation. The bare muscular chest, with its haze of dark hair, shouted for attention, but Bethany averted her eyes self-consciously, feeling too much like a voyeuse, and concentrated instead on Chad's face. His lashes were thick and spiky, framing those intriguing eyes that seemed to change their shade according to mood. Angry equalled dark with flashes of gold. Amused, and the eyes turned a shade softer, changing their shape slightly with a crinkling of the fine lines around the edges. Sensual? Bethany inhaled a careful breath and averted her thoughts. There was an indentation in his chin, almost hidden at the moment by a growth of dark stubble. His nose was long and straight, a good balance for the angular jawline and strong cheekbones ...

'It's a shame you're so ill, Bethany. I find I like it a great deal when you scrutinise me so completely.' Chad opened his eyes wide and gazed at the startled features with a slow, seductive smile. 'So what is the conclusion, eh?' he continued, propping his head up with one muscled arm. 'Do I pass muster?'

Bethany felt as if she had been caught doing something far worse than merely looking, as a flood of heat rushed from her neck to the roots of her hair. 'What... are you doing in this bed?' she enquired abruptly, in an attempt to divert some of her embarrassment back towards Chad.

'Sleeping, what else?' he replied, his mouth twisting attractively as he scanned her face. 'I'm no martyr; that chair became damned uncomfortable after a couple of hours.'

'You could have slept in another room,' Bethany croaked hoarsely. 'I didn't need constant surveillance, you know!'

'You credit me with too much compassion,' Chad informed her silkily. 'Keeping an eye on you had very little to do with it, I'm afraid! You see, this is the only bed in the house. I have, if my memory serves me correctly, nine bedrooms here, but unfortunately this is the only one that is in any way habitable at the present time.'

'So how... how long have you been awake?' Bethany demanded faintly, wishing she could drag her gaze from the far too attractive face.

Chad smiled lazily, his eyes crinkling at the corners just as she had imagined. 'Long enough! How do you feel?' he added lightly. 'You're looking kind of hot.'

'Not too bad,' Bethany muttered, turning away from him to reach for the glass of water and bottle of tablets beside the bed. 'I need some more penicillin. What time

is it?' she asked, after she'd swallowed the prescribed
dose and flopped back against the pillows. 'I'll have to
be getting back—the animals will need seeing to.'

Chad glanced at his gold wristwatch and then threw
back the cover and raised himself from the bed in one
fluid movement. 'Just after nine. Not that that is rel-
evant in any way because you won't be going anywhere.'

'But——!'

'Nothing's changed. Remember what I said to you last
night, Bethany?' he added, standing before her with his
arms folded across the broad naked chest in a stance of
pure male vibrancy. 'No buts allowed. Lie back, relax,
and quit worrying about your herd. I will do whatever
is necessary.'

'You?'

'Is it so impossible to pick up a few eggs and throw
down some corn?' Chad queried lightly, surveying the
worried frown that had immediately appeared on
Bethany's brow. 'Do I need some kind of certificate in
animal management or something?'

'The goats will need milking—you'll never be able to
do it,' she informed him anxiously.

'Now come on!' A smile twisted the firm mouth. He
looked across at Bethany's flushed face and his eyes
glinted fire. 'Don't you have any faith in my abilities?'

CHAPTER SIX

'I REALLY am not going to win this argument, am I?' Bethany whispered wearily.

Chad lifted his broad frame in a careless shrug. 'Not a chance! Now, I'm going to take a quick shower,' he announced, 'then I'll run you a bath.'

He emerged five minutes later from the *en suite* bathroom, dressed only in a towelling robe. Bethany watched in trepidation as he crossed the room towards her, felt shock and a thrill of excitement surge through her as he flicked back the cover and proceeded to lift her from the bed with all the infuriating ease of a man who had complete confidence in what he was doing.

'Presumably you have decided it's time for my bath,' Bethany muttered unsteadily. 'Don't I have a say in the matter?'

'No.' Chad swung her towards the bathroom door. 'You were very hot and sticky last night. A warm bath will make you feel much better.'

'I haven't lost the use of my legs, you know,' she replied irritably, conscious of the broad chest pressing against the thin fabric of her nightdress, conscious that there wasn't much in the way of a barrier between their naked bodies. 'I am quite capable of walking.'

'This way is much quicker.' Chad placed her on to a wicker chair in the large, airy bathroom and bent to turn off the gushing taps. 'There are plenty of oils and lotions along that shelf and there's another robe on the back of the door for you to change into. Will you be OK?'

Bethany glanced at the inviting pool of fragrant water and tried to work out how long it had been since she'd had a proper bath in such pleasant surroundings. She nodded silently.

'Good. I'll get dressed and then go down to the farm and play at Old Macdonald.'

'Chad!' He turned at the door and looked at her steadily and Bethany found herself colouring under his cool, scrutinising gaze. 'Thanks,' she murmured awkwardly, 'for... for looking after me like this.'

He shrugged. 'Think nothing of it—what else are neighbours for?'

The bath was heavenly: a hundred times better than her usual arrangement of boiling masses of water and filling the large tin tub in front of the stove at the cabin. Bethany just wished she felt better so that she could have enjoyed it more. But then, she reasoned, as she gingerly climbed out of the rapidly cooling bubbles, if she had been fighting fit she would never have found herself in this situation in the first place. Would she?

Bethany stood dripping on the cream tiled floor and struggled to find the energy to dry herself. She had stayed in the hot bath for far too long, a habit from the old days when careful timing late at night often meant the difference between coming to bed with Philip awake and aggressively drunk, or asleep and snoring like a baby, and now she was paying the price—her head felt light and peculiar and her body felt like lead.

'Bethany! Are you OK?'

She started at the sound of Chad's deep voice, close on the other side of the door, and lurched for the thick cream towel which was hanging over the back of the chair. 'Y-yes, I'm fine,' she replied faintly, far too faintly, for as she struggled against the sudden wave of blackness that threatened to take hold the door was suddenly wrenched open and Chad burst into the room.

'Bethany! Are you...?' He halted at the sight of her, watching without hesitation as she jerked the towel upwards to cover ineffectually her naked soapy body.

There was a long, intense silence. Bethany found herself rooted to the spot, unable to think or breathe, mesmerised by the compelling potency of Chad's lingering gaze.

'I didn't hear you reply,' he informed her finally, in a voice that was deep and rough-edged, full of smouldering tension. 'You've been in here a long time. I thought maybe——' he hesitated, and she felt a weakness consume her as his look covered every part of her '—something had happened to you.'

Bethany swallowed and shook her head silently, unable to drag her large, luminous eyes from the chiselled features, the smouldering expression. 'I'm all right,' she whispered.

Chad drew in a taut breath and let it out very, very slowly. 'So I can see,' he murmured, casting dark, provocative eyes down the silky golden length of Bethany's body.

His look thrilled her. Bethany felt a fierce sweet ache deep in the pit of her stomach and tried to ignore the need and the desire that had flared out of nowhere. She must not want him like this. She *must not*! It was practically asking for trouble all over again. Hadn't she suffered enough where men were concerned?

She tugged her towel upwards to cover her naked breasts and inhaled a deep breath. 'Did...did you find me something to wear?' she asked shakily.

He didn't move. She wondered if he had heard her. Then finally he said, 'There's a T-shirt on the bed.'

Bethany closed her eyes for a moment in something approaching despair. 'Could...could you get it for me?' she asked faintly, stepping back a little towards the wicker chair, gripping the arm for support.

Chad's brows snapped together at her movement, at the look of uncertainty on her face. 'It's all right. I'm not going to touch you!' he informed her with sudden harshness. 'There's no need to look quite so damn petrified! I didn't break the door down just so I could have my wicked way with you on the floor of the bathroom.'

Bethany released a quivering breath as Chad made his exit with a sharp click of the door, and closed her eyes in despair. It's not you I'm afraid of, Chad! she cried silently, shaking her head. Can't you see that? Can't you understand? It's me!

'I'll need to borrow some trousers as well.' Bethany took a deep, steadying breath and glanced across towards the window where Chad stood looking out. 'Just until I get to my place, I mean.'

He turned, thrusting his hands into the pockets of his jeans to survey Bethany almost abstractedly. 'What did you say?'

'I...I can't go home in just a T-shirt. I...' She hesitated and then added self-consciously, 'It was the middle of the night... I came without any underwear—remember?'

Dark brows drew together in a frown. 'Who says you're going anywhere?' Bethany gulped, looked confused, and said in a voice that was a little unsteady, 'But...but I can't stay here any longer. I'm...I'm an inconvenience——'

'Have I said that?'

His voice was harsh again. Bethany blushed. 'No, but——'

Chad moved towards her, thought better of it and turned back towards the window. 'Don't be ridiculous!' he retorted. 'There's no way I'm going to allow you back to that spartan shack while you're in this sort of state!'

'May I remind you that you are not my keeper, Chad Alington!' Bethany shot back, stung by his sudden change of mood, his cutting dismissal of her home. 'I decide where I go, what I do——'

'Not at the moment, you don't!' he interrupted tersely, facing her once more with an expression that defied disobedience. 'You've still got a temperature and you look absolutely worn out. Now do the sensible thing and get into that bed before I feel compelled to resort to physical restraint!'

'You...wouldn't?' Bethany's eyes were large and questioning.

Chad's dark brows drew together in a frown. 'Do you want to try me?' He looked as mad as hell.

She pursed her lips together in exasperation. She was too tired to think. He had told her to stay and she was too exhausted to argue. With an inward sigh of great relief, she slid thankfully between the sheets. He was right. She did still feel unwell: hot and tired and aching all over—it was a blessing to be able to lie down.

'Aren't you going to change?' Chad enquired bluntly, moving towards the bed to pick up the large white T-shirt. 'Surely that robe is going to be mighty uncomfortable in bed. Or do you think I won't be able to restrain myself?' he added coolly, holding out the garment towards her, watching Bethany's flushed expression with hard, impassive eyes. 'Clearly you expect the worst from me. Your look of fearful anticipation in the bathroom made that as clear as hell!'

'Please!' Bethany whispered, closing her eyes wearily. 'Please, Chad, don't be like this!' She gulped and swallowed painfully. 'How...how I looked just now...it wasn't the way you're imagining it... I'm not used to...to this...' She hesitated. 'Well, the way it is between us sometimes. Can't...can't you understand that?' Her voice trailed away and she waited nervously, half expecting one of Chad's sharp, cutting replies.

Nothing. She opened her eyes. The room was empty. Chad had gone.

Bethany managed to sleep for most of the day and by evening her throat felt a great deal better, still sore, but not with the same degree of agonising sharpness that she had experienced earlier.

She sat herself up in bed and leaned back against the pillows, glancing automatically towards the window, staring at the beautiful blue sky with unseeing eyes. Her mind was in turmoil. Bethany knew she should be making the effort to get up and leave, but somehow, despite everything, despite the fact that she knew this was an impossible situation, she found herself not wanting to make the move.

Eventually Bethany threw back the bedcovers and swung her legs on to the polished wooden floor. It would be best if she left now. What was the point in prolonging this dreadful limbo?

She padded barefoot over to the window and opened it wide, breathing in the warm evening air, her eyes automatically drawn, first along the cliff top towards her own small wooden cabin, then out towards the compelling expanse of blue-green sea.

'Evidently you must be feeling better.'

Bethany kept her eyes on the view and forced her voice to sound light and as normal as possible. 'Yes. Much better, thank you. Good as new, in fact,' she lied, after a hesitant pause. 'I really think I should be getting back home now.' She swung round and saw to her surprise that Chad was holding a large tray laden with any number of covered dishes.

'You must be hungry.' He set the food down on to the large oak chest at the foot of the four-poster bed and moved across to the window to clear the small round table that was positioned next to where Bethany stood. 'As you're already up and about, we can dine here. The view's particularly stunning this evening, don't you think? Very clear and sharp.'

Bethany glanced at Chad's inscrutable expression and forced herself not to care that he had evidently gone to a lot of trouble. 'I told you, I was just about to leave,' she murmured.

Chad straightened up and pierced Bethany's confused expression with a glance that told her she was wasting her breath. 'Sit down and eat!' he commanded. 'You need fattening up—I've remembered what the doctor said about eating more, even if you haven't. And I can assure you that the food has been chosen and prepared with your throat in mind.' He carried the tray to the table and then pulled out a chair for Bethany, waiting with unnerving patience until she had reluctantly seated herself.

'Do you always bully people?' Bethany enquired stiffly, trying hard not to notice how delicious the mouth-watering selection of dishes looked as he lifted the various lids.

'Of course!' Chad reached over to the bed and handed Bethany the thick towelling robe she'd worn earlier. 'Here, you'll need this. We don't want you catching your death of cold on top of everything else, do we?'

'Thank you.' She took it from his outstretched hand, aware of his slightly sarcastic tone, careful to avoid his touch, and slipped it hurriedly over the far too short T-shirt, tying it securely at the waist, promising herself that as soon as this meal was over she would definitely leave.

'You like pasta, I hope?' Chad asked crisply, handing Bethany a plate loaded with tagliatelle in a chicken and mushroom sauce.

'Yes.' Bethany smiled nervously and sniffed in appreciation, guilt washing over her because he had evidently gone to so much trouble. 'It smells wonderful! How long have you been slaving away at this?'

'Oh, hours!' Chad drawled. 'You've no idea! Actually,' he added flatly, 'I have a woman who comes in from the village once a day. She's the excellent cook—not my forte, I'm afraid.'

'Oh, I see.' Bethany spooned in a mouthful of food and tried not to feel disappointed. Somehow the thought of Chad labouring away in the kitchen, preparing the meal for them both, had conjured up a pleasant warm feeling inside.

'Is it that good?' Chad enquired, watching with a faintly amused glance as Bethany closed her eyes to savour the full effect of the pasta.

Bethany raised dark lashes and forced her fork to slow down. 'It's ... very nice,' she informed him with careful neutrality. 'I didn't realise I was quite so hungry.'

'You must be sick to death of carrots and cheese—or whatever it is that you live on,' Chad announced, pouring sparkling mineral water for them both.

Bethany lowered her head and concentrated on her food, disconcerted by the mocking gaze. 'It's a little more than that,' she murmured stiffly.

'But not so much that anyone would notice,' he drawled. 'A few other vegetables, eggs, bread. Your food cupboards at the shack aren't exactly bulging with tasty treats, are they?'

Bethany's green eyes jerked up and met his. 'You've been snooping around!' she accused. 'How dare you——'

'You asked me to see to your animals—remember?' Chad replied sharply. 'I had to find something to collect the eggs in.'

'Oh, and that conveniently meant you had to open every damn cupboard and drawer, I suppose!' Bethany retorted.

'You should make sure you consume enough good food, Bethany, especially as you lead such a physical life,' Chad continued, totally unperturbed by her simmering outrage. 'By the way,' he added smoothly, 'that larger goat of yours was an absolute devil. The damn thing wouldn't stand still!'

'She can be naughty,' Bethany admitted distractedly, her mind still thinking about how much of her privacy Chad Alington had so casually invaded. 'You've got to be firm.'

'Oh, I was that all right!' Chad replied drily.

'What did you do?' Bethany snapped suspiciously, suddenly alert. 'You didn't hurt her, did you?'

Dark eyes probed hers. 'You think I would?'

She inhaled a breath and shifted her gaze. 'It wouldn't surprise me,' she muttered. 'After all, you're used to violence. It used to be an integral part of your life, didn't it?'

'Maybe it did,' Chad responded tersely. 'But that doesn't mean I go around harming defenceless animals, whatever you so clearly would like to believe! I was about to say that I gave her enough food to sink a ship, just so she would stay in one place long enough for me to milk her!'

'Oh, great!' Bethany flared. She flung down her fork with a clatter. 'Waste all my animal feed, why don't you? As if I haven't got enough to worry about!'

'Eat your food and stop being so ridiculous!' Chad instructed. 'We are supposed to be having a civilised meal together.'

'Well, maybe I'm just not capable of that!' she snapped. 'Maybe sharing a meal with you puts me off my food!' It was a pretty big insult. Bethany's hand trembled a little as she reached out for her glass of water.

'What exactly is wrong with you all of a sudden?' Chad demanded.

'I don't like people poking their noses into my home,' Bethany replied shakily. 'You had no right!'

'I was searching for a basket for the eggs and a jug for the milk!' Chad explained through gritted teeth.

He was exercising great control—Bethany had to give him that, while she, of course, was behaving particularly badly. She pressed the palm of her hand against her hot head and knew she should apologise.

There was a moment of charged silence. Bethany raised her eyes to the cold, metallic face. 'Sorry...' She released a weary breath. 'I didn't...I didn't mean any of that.'

'OK.' The hard expression softened a fraction. 'Try and relax, Bethany. You're too tense.'

'I know.' Her voice was quiet.

'Shall we start again?'

Bethany drew a deep, calming breath and matched Chad's smile of compromise with a shaky one of her own. 'Please.'

'So tell me,' he instructed, after several moments of remarkably companionable silence, 'about the way you live your life. No need to look defensive, Bethany—I'm not trying to pry,' he added smoothly. 'Just interested. I began to understand about the attractions of your way of living while I was doing my bit at your place. It's very peaceful and secluded there, isn't it? You really could be back in the nineteenth century—if it weren't for the truck, of course,' he added with a quick smile. 'Are you totally self-sufficient?'

'Not really, but I do my best,' Bethany replied cautiously. 'I grow enough vegetables for myself and I have the eggs and the milk so I can make cheese and butter. I have to buy in coal for the stove from time to time, and feed for the chickens, and that means using the truck, which means petrol——'

'When it's working,' Chad cut in.

'Yes.' Bethany picked up her glass and took a mouthful of cool water to soothe her aching throat.

'And is it a good life?'

'Good? Well...well, yes of course!' she answered, after the slightest hesitation. 'There's a feeling of great reward, satisfaction, when simple, honest tasks are completed. Life is much less...much less complicated.'

'It was complicated before?'

Bethany saw the stunning eyes darken a little as Chad's gaze rested on her face. She licked her suddenly dry lips and after a long moment nodded. 'Yes.'

Was he going to pursue it? Bethany waited in trepidation and breathed an inward sigh of relief when Chad only murmured, 'It must be difficult living from hand to mouth like you do. Don't you find it hard?'

'At first maybe I did,' Bethany replied, considering. 'I didn't have much of an idea how to go about anything in the beginning, just got it into my head that this was a good way to lead my life. I read a few books, thought that would be enough— it wasn't, of course,' she added with a rueful smile. 'But gradually I learned how to live on very little.'

'You don't get any help?'

Bethany's forehead crinkled into a frown. 'What sort of help?'

Chad shrugged. 'You're out of work, living on practically nothing. I would have thought a visit to the social security department wouldn't go amiss.'

'Oh, no...no, I don't think so——'

'But you have tried, surely?' Chad's expression showed puzzlement. 'It may not be much, but I'm sure you'd be entitled to something. Even if it's only in the form of a grant to install a proper bathroom, instead of that quaint but rather outdated form of convenience you've got now. You *have* tried, haven't you?' he persisted.

'No...no, I haven't.'

'What?' His narrowed gaze swept over her.

'Look, could we forget all about this subject,' Bethany replied, an anxious frown creasing her forehead. 'I don't really want to talk about it.'

'I'd always come with you, if you're nervous about making a visit——'

'It's not that! Could you please just drop the subject—OK?' Bethany pushed her plate away and stood up. 'Now, thank you for the food, but I really think I should be getting back,' she continued, refusing to look at the probing dark eyes that were boring into her. 'The animals will need seeing to again.'

'They're already bedded down for the night, so you've nothing to rush back for. Besides which,' Chad murmured very quietly, 'you haven't finished your meal.'

'I'm not hungry!' She glared at him, summoning as much anger as she could muster for this arrogant, interfering man, who persisted in unsettling her with words...looks...touches...and finding, with a surprise that shook her, that it was difficult to feel any *hate* for him at all... Something else maybe, but not hate...

'Bethany.' His voice was gently persuasive as he rose from the table. 'There really is no need to be like this.' He placed a large tanned hand on her cheek and looked deep into the watery green eyes. 'If you don't want to talk about it, then that's fine by me.'

Bethany gulped. 'It is?'

Chad nodded. 'Of course.'

'And if I do?' Her voice was barely a whisper as she fought back the hot tears.

'Are we talking about going to the social security office now, or something else?' His voice was deep and magnetic, his eyes dark and desperately intense.

Bethany's lashes glistened with moisture as she raised her face to his. 'Something...else.'

'I'm listening.'

The room was quiet. Far off in the distance the soothing sound of the waves crashing on to the shore could be heard. Bethany kept very still. Suddenly she wanted to tell him; the urge to unburden herself of the agonies of the past was quite overwhelming.

'It...it upsets me,' Bethany murmured, glancing out of the window towards the sea, finding herself unable to look into the rugged attractive face a moment longer for fear of making a complete fool of herself. 'I've never spoken about it to anyone. I'll make a fool of myself...'

'Try.'

'I didn't have anyone, you see,' she continued, attempting to school her voice into sounding matter-of-fact. 'My mother died when I was young. No other close relatives, no sisters or brothers...just a couple of old aunts...and they wouldn't have understood...or been able to help...' Bethany swallowed and glanced towards Chad, saw the hard jawline and dark eyes intent on her face and looked away again. 'Have you—anyone close, I mean?'

'A sister, in Australia. No one else.'

'Do you see her?' Bethany asked, fighting against the tightness in her throat.

'Not for a long time.' Chad's voice was deep, relaxed. Bethany wished she could feel that way too.

'You should,' she replied croakily. 'Flesh and blood—it counts for a lot. You realise that when things go wrong, when you've got no one there to turn to.'

'What went wrong for you?' Chad murmured quietly. Bethany shook her head and pressed her lips together. Her eyes were filling up with tears. 'Tell me, Bethany,' he urged gently. 'At least give it a try.'

'I can't!' Her response was a strangled cry, wrenched out, straight from the heart. 'I thought maybe I could, but it's not that easy! Look——' she spun away '—thank you for looking after me, but I've really got to go!' She moved blindly, knocking the edge of the table in her haste.

'Bethany!' Chad's hands were gripping her arms, steadying her, preventing her from leaving. 'Tell me!'

'I can't!' She shook her head wildly, aware that the tears were coursing down her cheeks unchecked. 'You don't understand!'

'Well then, make me!' Chad's broad frame was blocking her way. She heard the deep, insistent tones. 'For God's sake, Bethany! This can't go on! Look at the state you're in!'

'I'll be all right!'

'Like hell you will!' He manoeuvred her unsteady frame over to the window, leaned her gently back against the wall. 'Bethany, I want to help you.' Both hands relinquished their hold on her arms and came up to stroke back the long silver strands of hair from her face. 'Let me help you.'

Bethany closed her eyes and tried not to sob. 'I'm so...so miserable!' she confessed chokingly.

'There's no need to be.' His voice was husky now, low and full of incredible vibrancy. Bethany felt the warmth of his body through the crisp denim shirt as it moved closer, quivered with awareness as one hand slid from her face to caress the long, slender arch of her neck, teasing back the thick folds of the towelling robe to reveal the thin T-shirt beneath. 'No need at all...'

His mouth covered hers in a long, slow, lingering kiss. Bethany closed her eyes and struggled against the deep spiral of awareness that was moving through her body. She wanted so much to wrap her arms around the broad shoulders, to enjoy the absolute command of the rugged frame that was moving closer with every second that passed, but still something held her in check. She

shouldn't be allowing this to happen...she shouldn't...
Chad wanted to blot out her pain for a short while, but
that wouldn't solve a thing. Afterwards, when it was
over, she knew she would still have to face the loneliness
of her life without him...

His kiss deepened. She felt him stir against her, felt
the pressure of his muscular thighs as Chad's body
moved against her own. His hands were slow and oh,
so gentle, travelling to the belt at her waist with unhurried ease, parting the robe very carefully, inch by inch,
as his mouth continued to work its magic. Spellbound,
Bethany found herself accepting at first and then posi-
tively inviting the sensual thrust of his tongue as it plun-
dered the moist depths. As if in a dream she felt her
arms gripping his shirt, clutching the fabric in a growing
desperation as he continued to hold and caress her body.

She shivered as he touched her. Wondered, in a crazed,
blind sort of way, if this was really happening. Marvelled at the way this man could make her feel...as if
she had taken a powerful drug, hardly aware of her surroundings, dizzy with physical need...

'I'm here for you...' His words were husky against
her lips. Bethany felt his arms tighten around her body
and then he was lifting her off her feet and carrying her
over to the huge, four-poster bed, laying her gently back
against the richly woven coverlet.

She glanced up at the ruched canopy overhead and
felt herself grow cold, felt the panic and the memories
of other times, many other situations sweep over her.
For one awful split-second the man that was leaning over
her wasn't Chad any longer but Philip, and in that instant she felt all the old repulsion flooding back, all the
old terror and fear.

'No!' She pushed with all her might against the bands
of steel that held her, struggling like a woman suddenly

and fearfully possessed. 'No!' Her cry rang out loud and sharp in the room as she began to fight to free herself. 'Leave me alone!'

'Bethany?' The voice was deep and disbelieving as she continued to struggle wildly. 'What's the matter? What is it?'

She rolled away from Chad's invincible frame as he released her and scrambled to her feet panting violently. *I am mad,* she thought, her pulses thudding violently as she ran for the door. What on earth is happening to me?

CHAPTER SEVEN

'DON'T touch me!'

Bethany had made it as far as the corridor before Chad reached her. He caught hold of her arm and spun her around to face him.

'Care to tell me just what that was all about?' he demanded grimly. 'Well?' He dragged her closer towards his towering body when Bethany looked away. 'One minute we're getting somewhere, the next—pow!' He made an explosive gesture with his hand.

'It...it wasn't right!' Bethany tried to tug her arm free but Chad wasn't having any. 'Let me go! I want to go home!'

'What wasn't right?' He threw her a mystified look, ignoring Bethany's futile struggles. 'What are you talking about?'

'Just forget it!' Bethany croaked, aware that his expression was, if that were possible, even more daunting. 'Just let me go and forget it!'

'What wasn't right?' he persisted fiercely. 'Tell me, Bethany!'

'I don't have to explain anything to you!' she flared defensively. 'Not a thing!'

'Well, I think you do!' Chad gritted, drawing her closer to his daunting male physique. 'For hell's sake! What do you think I'm made of—granite? Just exactly how much self-control do you think I possess?'

'I...I don't know! Please, stop raising your voice. Leave me alone! Can't you see what you're doing to me?'

'And what about what you're doing to me?' Chad gritted. 'Or doesn't that count?' The dark eyes were narrow and hard. 'Don't I have any emotions? What do you think I am, an automaton or something?'

'I...I don't know...' Bethany shook her head. 'I...I haven't thought about——'

'Anyone else except yourself?' Chad threw her a scathing look. 'Well, I have, and I think it's time you came out from behind that shield. I think it's time you gave a little. Did away with that precious aura of over-sensitivity and mournfulness. Faced up to the fact that life is all around you, waiting to be enjoyed.'

'And that means going to bed with you, presumably!' Bethany retorted unsteadily. 'Can't you see that...that I wish I'd never set eyes on you?'

'All I can see is one hell of a mixed-up woman!' Chad thundered. 'A woman who uses anger and hysteria to hide behind. A crazy woman who refuses to accept that she needs help——'

'Not that sort of help!' Bethany cut in. Her voice, her whole body, was shaking like a leaf in a force ten gale, but she wouldn't, couldn't let him get away with accusations like that. 'Never that sort of help! How convenient and utterly predictable it was for you to use my so-called problems as an excuse for sex! How clever of you to pretend to understand, to pretend to help, when all along the only thing you had on your mind was...was that...that act!'

'You didn't seem to mind at the time,' Chad informed her through gritted teeth. 'And by the way, "that act" as you refer to it, is normally called making love, or haven't you heard?'

Bethany felt her heart constrict painfully. 'Making love! Sex! It's all the same thing!' she snapped wildly.

'Just a man pursuing his urge to procreate—and if he can dominate at the same time, so much the better. Now let go of my arm!'

'My God!' Chad's voice was quiet now as he gazed down into Bethany's feverish face with eyes that held disbelief. 'You really do have one hell of a problem, don't you?'

'Maybe I do, but I think I can deal with it a whole lot better on my own. I was doing fine, just fine until...until you barged into my life with your over-sized ego and started ruining everything!' Bethany stormed. 'I hate you! Do you understand that? I hate you?'

'Well, well! Excuse me, I'm sure. I didn't realise I was interrupting something!'

Bethany jolted at the sound of the voice below. She turned slowly, feeling sick over the dreadful scene with Chad, her nausea rising further as she caught a glance through the banisters of Theo, shimmering like a Christmas decoration in an outfit of black and gold, standing in the tiled hallway below.

'What are you doing here?' Chad's tone was daunting as he moved to the top of the stairs and cast cold eyes in Theo's direction.

'Now, Chad!' Theo simpered. 'What sort of a welcome is that?'

'The sort of welcome I reserve for people who enter my house uninvited,' he replied sharply. 'I don't re-member hearing you knock.'

'Oh, I did, darling!' Theo moved to the bottom of the staircase and looked upwards towards them both, her eyes gleaming malevolently at Bethany who stood rooted to the spot, pale-faced and breathing unsteadily. 'You obviously just didn't hear me. Would you like me to retreat until you've finished your...er...conversation?' she asked innocently.

'Don't be clever, Theo—it's not your style!' Chad moved towards Bethany. 'I suggest you get back in the bedroom,' he growled under his breath. 'I'll get rid of Theo.'

'Don't bother!' Bethany shot back unsteadily, forcing her face to assume a mask of complete dislike. 'I don't think you and I have anything else left to say to one another, do we?'

Chad's eyes transfixed her face for a second and Bethany felt herself tremble beneath his intimidating appraisal. 'You know, maybe I've misread you all along,' he drawled. 'Maybe you're one hell of a mixed-up woman who's more than capable of taking care of herself.' He moved forward and Bethany felt rather than saw every ounce of tension in his large frame. 'Either way, don't doubt for a minute that I will always get the better of you, that if I so desired I could take you back into that bedroom and——'

She felt herself grow cold. '*Rape*?' The word was a whisper of shock.

Chad shook his head. 'Oh, no! Give me a little more credit. Nothing quite so crude or unrefined as that.' A menacing amusement revealed itself in his expression. 'Here, let me show you what I had in mind...'

One swift movement and she was in his arms. Another, and she felt his lips burning, scorching hers, moving with persistent and long-practised ease, managing, despite every mad thing that had happened, to light the flames of desire all over again.

He released her finally and Bethany saw the small smile of satisfaction as he lifted his head, knew with every part of her body and soul that what he said was the truth. 'Get the idea?' he drawled.

'I hate you!' she hissed.

'Change the record, why don't you?' he retorted bitingly. 'That one's wearing a bit thin for my liking!'

He turned abruptly, his dark gaze fixing on Theo, who had evidently watched the scene with a great deal of astonishment and displeasure. 'So, what is this—a social call?' he enquired tersely.

'Of course, darling!' The fuchsia mouth was forced into an alluring smile. 'We have a date.'

'Since when?'

'Since last week.' Theo gave him an exasperated look and placed a slender foot on the lower stair, revealing a provocative expanse of black-stockinged leg. 'We were going to try that very new—and very expensive—restaurant, remember?'

Chad sauntered to the bottom of the staircase and lounged against the wall, regarding Theo in brooding silence for a moment, allowing his masculine gaze to linger on the thigh-length split, the low, practically all-revealing cleavage.

Clearly Bethany had been forgotten. She stood in a daze of shock and fatigue and watched, wondering if she could possibly cope with any more.

'I don't think your outfit is quite right for a respectable restaurant, Theo,' Chad drawled, moving closer, effectively—perhaps deliberately—blocking Bethany's escape route.

She watched with an agonising lurch, a foolish, masochistic curiosity overwhelming her as Chad leaned forward and placed a hand on the black-stockinged thigh, felt a painful raw ache inside as he continued the deliberate humiliation and drew Theo towards his body with a rough jerk to kiss the carefully tanned neck.

'Bethany and I were just having a little disagreement about sex,' he drawled, lifting his head after a moment, not looking in her direction but keeping his gaze fixed on Theo's avid face. 'The physical pleasure of the body without the complication of emotional ties. We're past masters at it, aren't we, Theo?' A grim curve twisted the hardened mouth as Chad flicked a glittering gaze in Bethany's direction. 'Do you see any resemblance here to what we experienced earlier?'

There was none. Theo, clearly aware of the underlying currents, but not understanding what was going on, managed to look triumphant; Chad merely looked bored and a little disgusted—with himself, with Theo or with herself? Bethany wasn't sure which.

'I don't have to stay here and watch this!' Bethany felt misery rising in her throat. 'I don't!' She flew down the remaining stairs on legs that felt like jelly and pushed past the two of them.

Her coat and trainers were by the front door and she grabbed at them wildly, not stopping to put them on until she had wrenched open the heavy front door and slammed it behind her again.

The evening was warm and beautiful but she didn't notice any of it. All she could think about was Chad. All she could feel was the pain inside, tearing away at her. She ran down the track towards her cabin as if the hounds of hell were at her heels, sobbing uncontrollably.

How could he be so cruel? How could he do that to her? She hated him! She hated him!

By the time she reached the cabin door, frustration and misery had consumed her completely. Blindly she turned the handle and stumbled inside. Not pausing to take off her coat, she headed for the door to her bedroom, flung herself down in a distraught heap and cried herself to sleep.

When she next awoke it was the middle of the morning. Bethany stared at the clock on the painted chest of drawers and marvelled at the fact that she should have been able to sleep for so long.

She moved stiffly and sat up. Her throat felt pretty dreadful, a cross between sandpaper and a drawer full of knives, and her head wasn't a lot better either. She swallowed gingerly, discarded her crumpled coat and forced herself to her feet. Like a person stranded in a desert for too long, she stumbled out through the bedroom door in search of water.

The sight of Chad sitting at the small oak table, writing industriously, shocked her into stillness. She watched as he wrote, felt a constriction twist painfully in her chest as her eyes locked upon the dark, dynamic figure clad in light-coloured trousers and a rust-coloured polo shirt.

After several agonising seconds he looked up and saw her watching him. For a moment neither of them spoke. Finally Chad broke the silence. 'You look awful.'

Bethany struggled to find her voice. When it appeared it was little more than a husky croak. 'No thanks to you.' She drew the towelling robe, *his* robe, closer around her body, conscious that she felt cold and hot all at the same time again and not sure whether it was due to fever or the unexpected sight of Chad. 'What...?' She swallowed again, wincing as the knives dug into her throat. 'What are you doing here?' She had wanted to sound harsh and aloof, but it was difficult with such pain.

'I'll get you a drink.' Chad rose from the table and filled a glass from the tap. 'Here.' He held it out towards her, his eyes dark and impenetrable on Bethany's pale face.

Slowly she reached out and accepted the glass, raising it to her parched lips. 'I asked you a question,' Bethany continued more strongly. 'You've got no right to barge in here as if you own the place!'

Chad moved back towards the table and picked up the piece of paper he had been writing on. 'I was just leaving you a note,' he explained neutrally. 'Do you want to read it?'

'No!' Bethany threw him an angry glance and took another mouthful of water. 'If that was some sort of an apology, you can forget——'

'It wasn't.' One large hand screwed the paper into a tight ball in front of her.

'Would you please leave!' Bethany persisted shakily, moving towards the door, working hard at keeping her countenance level. 'I have a lot to do today.'

'No, you haven't,' Chad informed her briefly, watching with a cool expression as Bethany wrenched open the door, allowing a flood of sunlight and fresh sea air into the cabin.

'What?' She drew confused brows together and tried not to be affected by the sight of Chad, standing large and indomitable, his arms folded across the broad muscular chest, only a few feet from her.

'You've got nothing to do,' Chad repeated tersely. 'I've seen to the animals and brought in enough fuel for the stove to last you for the rest of the day. That's what I was writing about.'

'What? Why?'

The blunt questions, her ungrateful tone, didn't faze him as she had hoped they would. He scrutinised her for a moment before answering. 'Because you're unwell.'

'And are you referring to my physical state now, or my mental one?' Bethany shot back waspishly. 'I'm a crazy woman, aren't I? Probably certifiable as far as you are concerned. After all,' she continued, glaring at the taut, dark features, 'I didn't fall completely for those often-practised charms of yours, did I? How was Theo last night, by the way? Good? A *real* woman?'

'You don't want to know, do you?' His voice was calm, but she could see a difference in his expression. Just the slightest hardening of the mouth, the tiniest stiffness around the strong jawline that told her she had hit the mark.

'Oh, but why not?' Bethany replied, warming to her theme, driven by a masochistic urge that made her want to suffer even more than she was already. 'After all, I might learn something! You, like all men, clearly found her quite irresistible—that tarty look, such a turn-on!'

'I haven't slept with Theo since that day I rescued you from the sea!' Chad thundered. 'Whether you believe it or not—that's up to you. Now, I've brought your penicillin.' Chad, with an obvious look of disgust, turned sharply from her to place the small brown bottle on the table. 'You've missed a couple of doses, so I suggest you take the next two tablets straight away. There's some vegetable soup on the stove for later. I made it myself so I don't know what it's going to taste like.' He moved towards the door and glanced down into Bethany's cold, immobile face, his dark eyes glinting fire. 'Get some rest!' he ordered. 'You look fit to drop. I'm going outside to work on the truck.'

He spent most of the day outside. Bethany, feeling more exhausted than she would have believed possible, sat in the rocking-chair with a thick rug over her knees and simply slept or stared out to sea.

She tried desperately not to think—but of course it wasn't that easy. Her awful, emotional display of wild temper earlier made her cringe now to think about it. He had made soup for her. Bethany glanced across towards the stove and felt confusion wash over her. Why was he bothering? Guilt? She shook her head slightly and sighed. Chad Alington wasn't the type to experience such an emotion. A sort of stubborn persistence, then? That was perhaps nearer the mark. A personalised code of conduct that made him do what he considered to be, at any rate, the right thing? Or perhaps it was pity? She considered this new idea for the first time. In his eyes she was surely an object that deserved a good amount of that: a lonely deranged young woman, living the life of a hermit, refusing to allow herself to surrender to his well-practised charms... Oh, yes, pity. 'You have one hell of a problem.' That was what he had said. Did she? Did she *really*?

The hinges of the gate creaked and she looked up expectantly, her heart turning over automatically, as she saw Chad striding down the path.

The light on this hazy afternoon was soft and subdued, still warm through the open window, heavy with the mingled scent of the jasmine that twined around the door and the distinctive smell of the sea.

She watched as he approached and quickly shoved away the ridiculous notion that maybe, somehow, the two of them might be able to forget their differences and start over again, for he looked purposeful and still as grim as hell.

'How are you feeling?'

His voice was as brisk as she had expected. She hated the fact that it mattered to her. She hated the fact that when his dark eyes scanned her pale, unattractive face and worn-out body, all wrapped up like an aged grandma, it mattered—it mattered so much it hurt.

Bethany matched her tones to his and replied in one single, frosty syllable. 'Fine.'

'Do you need anything?'

She steeled herself mentally. There were any number of things she desperately needed—but not from this man, never from someone like him.

She switched her gaze to the window and looked out towards the sea once more. 'No, thank you, I'm fine.'

'So you keep saying.' He regarded her broodingly. 'I've fitted the parts to the truck and changed the oil. Oh, and there were a couple of fence posts loose. I fixed those too.' He moved across to the stove and lifted the lid of the copper saucepan that had been sitting there untouched all day. 'You haven't risked the soup. Did you think it looked that bad?'

Bethany watched as he leaned nonchalantly against the table with his hands thrust into his pockets, and shrugged stiffly—an attempt at casualness that didn't quite come off. 'I haven't felt particularly hungry.'

She saw his eyes darken with exasperation. 'Well, you should have forced yourself.' He glanced briefly at the flash of gold at his wrist. 'I'll heat it up and you can have some now.'

'I don't want any of your damned soup!' Bethany flared. 'Just go. Leave me in peace. You've wasted enough time here as it is. I'm perfectly all right.'

She hadn't meant it to be like this. Between fitful dozes, she had been aware of him as he worked outside on the truck, had felt her heart quicken each time it looked as if he were going to come into the cabin. All day at the back of her mind had been the thought that when he came inside she would make amends for her bad behaviour. In unguarded moments she had found herself rehearsing her lines, imagining his responses in return ... hoping for some sort of divine intervention, a way out of the tangled mess and misery that she seemed destined to fall prey to...

She hard a sharp intake of breath and waited for him to storm out. I don't know why I'm acting like this! she wanted to yell. I'm sorry! Please, I don't want you to go!

He didn't, not immediately anyway, and she felt a flood of relief rushing through her.

'You are going to have something to eat, even if I have to force it into you,' he informed her grimly. 'And it might as well be some of this damned soup! And don't bother to say you're not hungry again,' he growled, turning on the stove with an angry twist, wrenching open a cupboard door with a jerk of irritation, 'because frankly I couldn't give a damn whether you are or not!' He slammed a bowl on to the table so hard Bethany thought it was going to break. 'Have you been taking your penicillin regularly?'

His voice was curt and harsh. Bethany looked down at her hands clasped tightly together in her lap, blinked back the sting of unexpected tears and nodded. 'Yes.'

'Well, that's something I suppose!' Chad answered forcefully. 'You do, it seems, possess at least a modicum of sense!'

'Not as much as I would like!' Bethany retorted swiftly, anxious that Chad should be unaware of how upset she really was. 'Otherwise,' she continued, in a voice that to her astonishment really did give little away, 'I wouldn't be allowing you in my home, making me to do things against my will, talking to me as though I'm some sort of child!'

'It's for your own good and you know it!' Chad replied curtly, ladling out a good proportion of the steaming vegetable mixture into the patterned bowl.

'And you expect me to feel grateful, I suppose!' Bethany flashed. 'For the work on the truck, the fence posts, your damned soup!'

'To be frank, I don't give a damn!' Chad replied, drawing a small side table close beside the rocking-chair and setting the bowl of soup and a spoon on to it. 'Now just be quiet and eat!'

She couldn't keep fighting him. With a sigh of exasperation, that left him in no doubt she was acceding to his request under sufferance, Bethany spooned the warming mixture into her mouth and found that she was hungrier than she had realised. The soup tasted surprisingly good and she was just beginning to feel fractionally better when, after the third or fourth mouthful, she saw Chad pull back his cuff and glance at his wristwatch again.

'Go!' she commanded instantly, her body rigid as she steeled herself for his imminent departure. 'You've got what you wanted—I'm eating and I've taken my penicillin like a good little girl! You've done your duty. So you can go away and enjoy yourself without having me hanging over your conscience!'

Chad's dark, glittering gaze spoke volumes. He folded his arms in a stance that portrayed all of his irritation. 'Don't you find this aggressive attitude of yours rather wearing?' he enquired curtly, scanning Bethany's taut, rigid face. 'I would have thought you'd have been better served saving your energies for getting well again.'

Bethany took a long, steadying breath and gripped her spoon very tightly. 'Just go,' she repeated. 'I don't need you here. Besides, I'm sure Theo will be getting extremely impatient.'

'Possibly she is!' Chad snapped as he moved towards the door. 'But as I have no plans to see her tonight, that has very little to do with me!'

'You really aren't...sleeping with her any more?' The hope...the plea had escaped from her lips before Bethany realised.

Chad turned and looked down at her, his gaze as inscrutable as ever. 'I've already told you once!' he gritted with merciless precision. 'I'm not in the habit of repeating myself.'

CHAPTER EIGHT

IT was several days before she saw him again.

Her throat had healed, but the raw, aching pain inside hadn't.

He looked as incredible as ever: khaki-coloured shorts and a crisp, short-sleeved shirt that billowed a little in the breeze.

Bethany pushed the sunglasses that were hanging on a string around her neck on to her nose and concentrated very hard on her weeding.

'Can I buy some eggs?'

She hesitated a moment and then swivelled around, steadying herself as she crouched among the vegetables with one hand on the garden fork. 'Sorry...no.' She saw the jaw tighten, the dark eyes narrow a fraction, and continued hurriedly. 'I don't mean you can't have any, just that I can't *sell* the eggs to you. They have to be certified by the ministry that they're free from salmonella before I can do that.'

'So you'll give me some?' Chad reached over the picket fencing and unhitched the gate. 'Are you sure you want to?' He strolled down the path between the neat rows of vegetables and halted a few feet away from her.

Bethany stood up as he approached and felt a sense of relief and immense pleasure; for some reason she had taken the trouble to braid her hair in one thick, shiny plait this morning, had slipped on a matching set of red shorts and a vest-style T-shirt instead of her usual outfit of ragged denims and any old shirt she could lay her hands on. She looked a hundred times better than the last time Chad had seen her. But did it matter? Did it really make any difference?

'A dozen—can you manage that?'

She nodded and collected her thoughts, aware as she glanced into Chad's face that the dark eyes were scrutinising her closely. She felt a rush of awareness at his gaze and gulped a shaky breath. 'Yes ... yes, I think so. Sometimes, when the hens are laying well, I have so many I don't know what to do. It's always the way. A dozen will be no problem. It will be a relief to off-load a few. I haven't been feeling particularly enthusiastic about scrambled eggs for breakfast every morning,' she continued unsteadily. 'Not since ... Well, not for the past few days ...' She broke off and looked away uncomfortably, not wanting to make any reference to her illness or the fact that she had simply not regained her appetite since his departure from her cabin six nights ago. 'I'll ... I'll just go and get a basket,' she murmured stiffly. 'I won't be a minute.'

'How's the throat?'

Bethany glanced around, eggs in hand, and saw that he had followed her inside the cabin, was lounging against the jamb of the door in a stance that oozed arrogant male vitality. 'Fine.'

'And the appetite?'

'Oh ... that's fine too,' she replied, with a forced attempted at casualness. *Liar!* she thought, you have to force every morsel past your lips.

She deftly filled the small wicker basket and turned towards Chad. 'Here you are,' she murmured quietly, holding out the eggs. 'I'm afraid they're a bit grubby; the hens aren't too careful where they lay.'

'It doesn't matter.' His eyes etched her face. 'I think we both know they were just an excuse anyway.'

'They were?' Bethany glanced up. Her voice was barely a whisper.

'Of course.' He reached out with a curve of his lips and accepted the basket, his gaze unflinching. 'I wanted to see you.'

She felt a surge of pure delight run through her, an intense feeling of pleasure that was almost a pain deep in the pit of her stomach. 'You did?'

She saw the smile broaden: a lazy curve that lifted the edge of the firm, sensual mouth, a sparkling of the dark eyes that made her feel as if she were floating on air. 'Yes.' He put the basket of eggs down on a nearby table. 'I want you to forget all this and come and spend some time on the beach with me. It's a lovely day.' Chad's gaze was sure and direct, clashing with eyes that were green and wide and full of uncertainty. 'No strings attached,' he informed her smoothly. 'No questions, no probing, no arguments. Just a pleasant day by the sea.' He paused. 'It's a perfectly straightforward invitation, Bethany. So there's no need to look quite so petrified.'

'I...I don't,' Bethany's voice sounded as uncertain as she looked. 'It's just a bit of a surprise, that's all. I mean, after the way——'

'After the way things have been between us, you don't feel particularly happy about spending any more time in my company, is that it?' Chad finished tersely.

This was it, then—ultimatum time. Everything about Chad's demeanour told her that if she refused this invitation, it would be tantamount to finishing their relationship on all levels. He would not be issuing second chances.

'If it helps remove that tortured expression, I'll add that we will have a couple of chaperons with us,' Chad informed her steadily.

Bethany switched her gaze to the rugged face and raised her brows in query. 'We will?'

'Yes, two youngsters I've promised to look after for the day. Brother and sister. I know it would be more fun for them if you came along. But of course,' he continued carelessly, shifting his position, making as if to go, 'if you've decided that you'd rather not have anything to do with me any more——'

'No, it's not that!' Bethany, aware that Chad was rapidly losing patience, that this was her last chance, made her decision. 'Please, I'd like to come!'

Chaperon or no chaperon, she wanted to be with him. It was as simple as that.

'So where are they, then?' Bethany had taken all of three minutes to grab a swimming-costume and a towel. She had considered food and something to drink, but decided that to bring along anything resembling a picnic would be as near to announcing that she hoped to stay all day with him as you could get.

Chad was waiting for her at the top of the cliff path. He turned at the sound of her voice, and then looked back towards the sea as she approached. 'You mean our trusty chaperons?' He shrugged nonchalantly and gazed down the steep path towards the beach, the corners of his mouth curving slightly. 'Oh, they've already made their way down by the looks of it. Eager devils. Masses of energy.'

'But surely you didn't let them out of your sight!' Bethany replied swiftly, her face contorting into a frown. 'The path's so difficult if you don't know it well, and besides they're only children. What on earth were you thinking of?' She looked down anxiously at the steep craggy rocks, and thought of all the times she'd so nearly missed her footing. 'Chad! Are you listening to me?' she enquired urgently, watching with a frown as he continued to stare out to sea. 'Come on. We'd better make sure they're all right.'

He caught her arm as she passed. 'Bethany, steady, for heaven's sake! I don't want you falling to your death!'

'But——'

'Trust my instincts,' he commanded evenly. 'I know they're all right—in fact I'm absolutely positive. Now, let me go first and take your time.'

'I have been down here before, you know!' Bethany retorted. 'I probably know these cliffs better than you!'

'Well then, you'll know how dangerous they can be if you're not concentrating properly!' Chad responded smartly, removing the bag which held her swimming things from her shoulder. 'I'll have that.'

'I can't believe you're taking this so calmly!' Bethany muttered, shaking her head in bewilderment as they began to descend the steep and twisting slope. 'Two children might be laid sprawled out on the rocks somewhere and you're being so damned casual about it... Oh!' Bethany's heart leaped into her mouth as her foot slipped without warning and she fell awkwardly forward, cannoning into Chad's solid back with a thud. She grabbed out automatically and found his strong arms instantly around her waist.

'Bethany, will you be careful!' he growled. 'You'll have us both over the edge!' He turned and Bethany, her body still trembling, from the shock of such close contact rather than her near fall, found her hand firmly and reassuringly clasped as Chad led the way with sure-footed ease to the bottom of the cliff.

'So where are they, then?' Bethany looked around worriedly, shading her eyes against the glare of the sun as she scanned the golden shoreline. 'I don't see them.'

'It's all right. No need to panic. They're here.'

She spun around and looked back towards Chad. He was bending down, trying to calm two glossy black Labradors, who were frisking around his legs and jumping up at him in a frenzy of pure delight. 'Where?'

'Here.' He picked up a smooth round pebble from the sand and threw it far out towards sea, watching as the two dogs raced away after it. 'Those are Bramble and Bruce.' He looked towards her and the firm line of his mouth curved into a wicked smile. 'Our chaperons for the day.'

Bethany inhaled deeply and then released a long, slow steadying breath. 'That was not fair!' she announced. 'You lied!'

'I did no such thing!' Chad met her gaze with a challenging one of his own. 'I maybe didn't tell you the complete truth, but——'

'Maybe?' Bethany shook her head in exasperation. 'You've brought me here under false pretences. Allowed me to believe that——'

'Do you want to go back, then?' His tone had hardened suddenly.

Bethany looked across at Chad's metallic expression and cursed the fact that she had managed to jump in with both feet again. She shook her head. 'No.'

'Well, stop making such a fuss, then.' He looked at her for a moment in silence, then added in a voice that was long on exasperation and pretty short on understanding, 'Lighten up a little, Bethany. I'm getting mighty fed up with the suspicious routine!' He moved to a cleft in the base of the cliffs and brought out a couple of cool boxes and a large canvas holdall. 'I don't know about you,' he murmured conversationally, handing one of the boxes to Bethany, who had walked over and was still debating whether to stay or to turn on her heel and abandon the whole foolish idea, 'but it's only mid-morning and I'm starving already. I watched Mrs Brooks, my housekeeper, load up some of the food and it looked absolutely marvellous. What do you say about an early lunch?'

'You knew I'd accept?'

Chad glanced sideways as they trudged along the smooth, flat beach. 'You don't like the idea that I can read your mind?' he queried with a mocking twist of his lips.

'Not particularly, no,' Bethany answered honestly. 'Tell me, are you always so sure of yourself?' she added waspishly.

'On this occasion, yes.' His eyes glittered across at her. 'Apart from the wonderful prospect of spending a day in my company,' he continued drily, 'there was always the draw of the beach. It's been several weeks since you were last down here—I know you've missed it.'

'I'm so transparent?' Bethany enquired lightly as she walked along beside the magnetic figure.

'About that—yes.' Chad stopped, placed the bags and boxes side by side on the sand and proceeded to unzip the holdall. 'Besides, you have lots of shells and pieces of curiously shaped driftwood about the cabin and, if you remember, you were here when I first saw you. It doesn't take a lot of working out, does it?' He spread out two rugs on the sand.

And you? she asked silently. Have you really figured out that I can't stop thinking about you? That no matter how hard I try I find myself drawn inexorably towards you?

'You look nice, by the way—that red outfit suits you, and so does the plait. Am I allowed to say that,' he queried, 'without you becoming all rigid and defensive on me?'

Bethany blushed and busied herself with helping to lay out the rug. 'Yes,' she murmured, conscious of his faintly mocking gaze, of the fact that such a throwaway compliment still had the ability to send a warm rush of pleasure through every part of her body. 'I suppose so.'

'You don't sound too certain.'

'I'm not sure I know what to do with compliments,' Bethany murmured. 'They always make me feel uncomfortable.'

'I'm sure that reply has deep psychological meaning, but we'll pass over that for now. Why don't you just smile and say thank you? That usually works well enough.' Chad pulled one of the cool boxes towards him and lifted the lid. 'Now, how about helping me to consume some of this food? I told Mrs Brooks you needed feeding up and it looks as though she's packed double everything.'

'I'm not really very hungry.' Bethany placed herself neatly on the edge of the rug and looked out to sea. 'I'll just have a bit of salad later on, if I may.'

'When did you last eat?'

'Earlier this morning, of course,' Bethany replied, glancing out towards the shoreline, watching the dogs with feigned interest as they frolicked in the surf.

'Don't be obtuse, Bethany!' Chad announced. 'It doesn't suit you. You know very well what I'm asking.'

'OK. Breakfast was four or five hours ago, around six!' Bethany declared irritably. 'Satisfied?'

'If you eat something, I might just be, yes,' he replied instantly. 'Until then, I'm afraid you will get no peace, no peace at all!'

He was half serious, half teasing. Bethany looked into the rugged, handsome features, watched as Chad unexpectedly made a funny face, and found her lips twitching into a smile. 'OK! Give me food, then!' she ordered, with mock severity. 'Anything to keep you from nagging me to death!'

'Me? Nag?' The dark head shook a little, and his expression was all innocence. He reached into the cool box and arranged a selection of mouth-watering dishes on the rug. 'Take your pick,' he instructed. 'I'll break open the beer—unless you would prefer something else? I have plenty of white wine, lager, mineral water...' He gestured towards the display of bottles, surrounded by chunks of ice, in the second cool box. 'Take your pick.'

Bethany licked her lips. 'A cold beer will be fine,' she murmured, helping herself to a crusty roll filled with salad and an appetising mixture of prawns and mayonnaise.

'You get points for quality *and* quantity,' Chad informed her, handing Bethany a brimming glass of ice-cool beer. 'The more you eat, the less like a sergeant major I become.'

'You seem to have an amazing talent for telling people what to do,' Bethany remarked lightly.

'Is that your polite way of saying I'm an overbearing, arrogant swine?' Chad enquired.

Bethany lifted her chin a little and found herself meeting the sparkling eyes with a light heart. This was how it was meant to be! Why hadn't it happened before? Why had they spent so much time fighting? 'Of course!' she agreed quietly. There was a long, electrically charged silence. She could feel, almost touch, the smouldering tension in the air between them. 'I'm sorry about how I behaved...the last time,' Bethany added quietly.

'You were ill,' Chad replied. 'Let's just leave it at that.'

She stole a nervous glance and saw his grim expression. 'You're making excuses for me, but we both know that that had nothing to do with it,' she persisted.

'Bethany, can't you understand? I don't want to talk about it! I behaved badly too. I'm still trying to forget how badly I behaved that evening...' His voice trailed to a halt. 'I'm sorry I humiliated you in front of Theo. I should never have done that. God knows what possessed me!' He stood up abruptly, pulling his crisp, white shirt over his head with a sudden, almost savage tug. 'Let's walk!'

Bethany looked away. She wasn't sure she could cope; this intense flash of mood, this huskily voiced apology, were having an incredibly disturbing effect. He had told her earlier to *relax*? Who was he kidding?

'Have you got something to wear on your head?' Chad enquired as Bethany rose self-consciously from the rug, brushing the crumbs of food from her shorts with over-zealous intensity, trying not to focus on the firmly muscled torso, with its haze of dark, dark hair. 'The sun's going to be pretty hot for the next hour or two and, as you're so fair, I think it would be wise to wear a hat.'

'No. No, I haven't,' she replied, thrusting her hands into the pockets of her scarlet shorts, turning to look anywhere except at Chad. 'But don't worry about me— I'm sure I'll be all right,' she continued unsteadily. 'I work outside in this sort of heat quite frequently. I'm...I'm used to it...'

'Wear this.' Her voice trailed away as Chad retrieved a white baseball cap from the holdall and, moving to stand before her, placed it over her corn-coloured head. 'You know I would never forgive myself if you contracted sunstroke. Shh!' He placed a finger on her lips and effectively halted the beginnings of a protest. 'It's possible, even in this country, so no arguments, or I'll have to start my sergeant major act again!'

'What...what about you?' Her voice was a shaky whisper. Did he know, she wondered, just what an effect simple actions could have on her? Could he see how difficult it was for her when his hands casually brushed against the strands of her hair? How impossible it was to appear in control of her senses when just one finger lightly grazed her lips?

'Forget me,' Chad instructed firmly. 'There's only one cap and I want you to wear it.'

She should have moved from him then, put some distance between his body and her own, but she didn't. Struck by the intensity in his eyes and the low vibrancy in his voice, she stayed where she was, rooted to the spot, aware that the tension that had been between them from the moment that she had set eyes on him this morning, the tension that was *always* there, was rising to a dangerously high level once again.

She waited, hardly daring to breathe, hardly daring to think, helpless as Chad's ebony eyes consumed her face. They were inches apart. She looked into the strong, rugged planes of his face, her pulses thudding violently, and almost willed something to happen.

'Shall we...?' He paused for a fraction of a second, and Bethany felt her heart lurch again at such tantalising timing. Was it deliberate? Bethany forgot how to breathe. Chad seemed to have forgotten how to talk. She felt a flush of awareness surge upwards from her neck, consuming her as his eyes continued to scour her face. What? *What*? A small voice clamoured inside. What shall we do?

'Shall we walk?'

It wasn't quite a slap in the face, but it stung just the same. Bethany wheeled around and began to stride away. She was shaking like a leaf. Angry with herself—*so* angry she felt she wanted to scream aloud in frustration, for allowing him the opportunity of making her feel a complete fool all over again. He was just playing games. He knew how she felt. He knew exactly.

'Bethany, wait!' He had caught up with her, his feet soundless on the dry, silvery sand. 'Stop acting like a child!'

'*What*?' She turned to face him, her expression one of helpless frustration.

'Don't look at me with those big, green innocent eyes!' Chad instructed sharply. 'You know what I'm talking about! So why the anger?' he demanded, his eyes glittering dangerously. 'What is it? Do you want me to forget my promises?' He shadowed her as she stalked along the beach, refusing, *unable* to answer. 'Do you want me to take you right here and now, is that it?'

The shocking bluntness of his words made Bethany halt in her tracks. 'How can you be so...so base?' she gritted. 'You're even more uncouth than I thought!'

Chad moved towards her, caught hold of her hand and dragged Bethany close against his body. 'We could do it,' he growled huskily, his dark eyes searing her face, making her feel weak, light-headed and apprehensive all at the same time. 'Here. Now. All you have to do is say the word. Nothing could be simpler——'

'Stop it!' Bethany's reply was little more than a strangled cry.

'Stop what?' Chad's gaze continued to rake the pale face. 'Stop the pretence? Is that what you mean? No, don't look away!' His fingers clasped her chin and tilted it firmly up towards his face. 'Don't you dare look away. Tell me, Bethany,' he commanded savagely. 'Tell me what it is you want. Because I sure as hell am sick of these games you continue to play.'

'*Me* play games!' The explosion of anger made her strong fleetingly. 'How *dare* you say that to me! How dare you!' She tried to pull away and realised instantly that the movement was absolutely pointless; his arms were like bands of steel around her body. 'Let me go!' she cried wildly. 'I must have been mad to agree to come here with you. Let me go! Let me go!'

She stumbled back as he released her, sprawling without any finesse on to the soft, warm sand at his feet, tears streaming down her face in unchecked torrents. 'I hate you, Chad Alington!' she sobbed, pounding the sand with a clenched fist. 'I hate you so much!'

'No you don't.' He had fallen on to his knees beside her, was gathering her shaking body into his arms. 'I may not know a great deal else, but I know that.' He held her close, discarding the cap that had fallen askew over her eyes, rocking her very gently, and Bethany, not surprised in the least by her total inability to resist him, found herself relaxing against the solid, masculine chest and releasing several days of pent-up emotion.

'You are a foolish girl, sweet Bethany,' he murmured against the strands of silvery hair, 'but then I am a very foolish man, so I guess we should call it quits...or else...' The sentence floated away, unfinished on the sea breeze. Finally, as her tears subsided and there was only the occasional heart-wrenching sob, he tilted her head away from his chest and looked down into the watery eyes. 'Feeling any better?'

Bethany struggled to speak. 'A...a little.'

'Do you want to go back?' His voice was neutral, flat and even, a total contrast to Bethany's thudding heart.

She shook her head. 'No.'

'Good.' He paused a moment, his face a mask of composure. Then he added softly, 'Whoever it was, he must have hurt you very badly.'

Bethany, stilled by the perceptive gaze, shuddered and closed her eyes. 'Yes.'

'Still hurts you?' His voice was deep, dark, deadly serious.

She nodded briefly. 'Yes...Chad...please——!'

'OK. I'm not about to pry.' His voice was a little rough. She felt his hands loosen their hold on her body and he rose to his feet, helping Bethany up with him. 'I think it would be best if I went for a swim,' he informed her laconically. 'Do you want to join me?'

'Isn't it a little soon after eating?'

Chad glanced at his watch. 'I don't think so. You cried for a long time,' he added, noting Bethany's surprised expression. 'Well?'

'I'll have to change,' she murmured. 'You go ahead. I'll...I'll join you later.'

He turned abruptly and walked down the beach towards the rippling waves. Bethany stood and watched as Chad executed a savage, thrusting dive and the smooth brown body disappeared beneath the foaming water.

She strolled back towards the rugs, glancing at intervals out towards the sea. Chad was still there, his arms slicing expertly through the water, going further and further away from shore, the dogs following behind in mad pursuit.

Slowly she changed into her swimsuit, not worrying too much about hiding beneath the beach towel in this private, sheltered cove as she discarded her underwear and slipped into the carefully chosen navy-blue two-piece that was the least revealing of all her costumes. Still pretty skimpy though, she observed anxiously as she stood up and adjusted the halter-neck top. Still far too skimpy...

She walked towards the sea, her eyes scanning the water. She could see the dogs, swimming to and fro, both with sticks in their mouths, but no sign of Chad.

The water, although as warm as it was ever likely to get after several weeks of continuous English summer sunshine, was still a shock to the system. Bethany hesitated, steeling herself against the cold as the waves broke against her shins.

'You may as well take the plunge and dive in. It's not going to get any better!'

Bethany looked up. Chad had appeared like a demigod from the waves, standing waist-deep in water, hands on hips, his dark hair, glossy and very black now, smoothed back from his face.

'I know you're right,' Bethany called, aware of the goose-bumps that had appeared all over her body, 'but that doesn't make it any easier.' She moved a few feet forward and retreated in disgrace when a wave higher than the others threatened to soak her.

'Stop being such a chicken! Are you going to come in or not?'

'Y-yes.' Bethany glanced at him warily as he moved towards her.

'So what date had you in mind?'

'I. . .' She stiffened and shrieked, jumping a little as another wave threatened her thighs. 'I just need to get used to it.'

'No time like the present!' Before she could escape them, Chad's hands were curving around her body. In an instant he had picked her up and was carrying her bodily through the waves.

'Oh, Chad! Oh, no! Pleeease!' It was too late. With a wicked smile at her squealing terror, Chad had thrown her, with one almighty swing, into the foaming sea.

She emerged gasping in shock, conscious that the water wasn't half as cold as she had imagined. 'You rotten devil!' she yelled. 'How could you do that to me?' With a cry of laughing fury, she lunged towards him, intent on revenge, splashing the blue-green water ineffectually in Chad's direction.

'I did it for your own good!' His mouth curved teasingly as he dodged out of the way. 'I can't remember the last time I've seen so many goose-bumps!'

'Stay in one place!' Bethany ordered, her face contorted with mock seriousness. 'You're too fast!'

'Why don't you take your feet off the bottom and actually swim?' Chad called, moving further out to sea. 'You never know, you might find it a lot easier to catch me!'

She did her best, but it was futile; Chad was far too strong a swimmer. Bethany, feeling exhausted and curiously much better after the light-hearted chase, spread her arms and floated on her back.

It was a gorgeous day: there wasn't a cloud in the sky. She closed her eyes and allowed her body to drift with the rhythmic swell of the sea.

'You're going out too far.' Chad's voice appeared out of nowhere, deep and calm beside her.

Bethany tilted forward and found to her surprise that her feet couldn't touch the bottom. She kicked vigorously in an attempt to tread water and found to her dismay, as she sank beneath the water, that she still hadn't mastered the art.

'Just relax and take it slowly,' Chad instructed, lifting her up. 'Move your arms in a semi-circle around your body and do the same with your legs. It's a lot easier than you think. You just need a little practice, that's all.'

'I haven't got time to practise!' Bethany spluttered. 'Save me! I'm drowning!'

He moved back towards her and she felt the reassuring feel of his hands around her waist, lifting her clear of danger. Hesitantly she placed her hands on the muscular brown shoulders for support. 'OK?' Bethany nodded and coughed up some sea-water. 'Go on, spit it out,' Chad smiled. 'I can assure you I won't be offended!'

Bethany leaned to one side and relieved herself of the nasty taste. 'That has got to be one of the most horrible feelings,' she announced unsteadily, 'suddenly finding yourself out of your depth.'

'Are you referring to swimming here, Bethany?' Chad murmured. 'Or life in general?'

She looked at the stunning eyes, the way they were studying her face, and thought for a moment before answering. 'Both,' she whispered.

'And how often have you been out of your depth?' he asked, his voice deep, his gaze intense and unflinching on her face.

'I am now.' Bethany swallowed. 'Can't you see?' She gulped a breath and then turned from him, throwing herself into a vigorous front crawl to swim away back towards the shore.

CHAPTER NINE

'I THINK I should be getting back to the cabin now.' Bethany hugged the warm towel close around her shivering body and watched a little apprehensively as Chad stretched out on the rug beside her.

'OK, if that's what you want.' He had closed his eyes. Bethany watched as he stretched his arms above his head and tried not to notice the rivulets of water that were streaming all over his tanned body. 'You know, I had a bet with myself,' he drawled sleepily, after a pause in which neither of them spoke. 'I watched you hurling yourself through the water and then running across the sand, and I mentally wagered a hundred pounds that you'd be running back to the cabin at the first possible opportunity.' He shaded his eyes with his hand and looked across at her. 'And I was right, wasn't I?'

'I...I just think it's time I was getting back, that's all,' Bethany replied defensively.

'Why?' Chad moved on to his side, propping his head up with one hand.

Bethany floundered under his scrutinising gaze. 'I'm...I'm feeling cold.'

'Change out of those wet things and you'll be fine. I've got a sweater in the bag that you can borrow.'

'The...animals—I need to keep an eye on them.'

Chad fell back, closed his eyes and smiled knowingly up at the sky. 'Oh, yes, of course!' he murmured drily. 'The faithful old livestock! You've been away all of——' he opened his eyes and glanced at his watch

'—all of two hours. I'm sure they'll be desperate for some attention!'

'Look! I don't have to explain myself to you!' Bethany responded angrily, hugging the towel around her knees. 'I don't!'

'Of course not. Anyway,' Chad added, 'I don't need any explanation—I know exactly what's going on in that beautiful head of yours.'

Bethany frowned fiercely, annoyed by his self-assurance, annoyed too because she felt pleasure at having any part of her labelled beautiful by Chad. 'I don't know what you're talking about!' she declared, reaching for her shorts and top. 'I just think it's time I was getting back, that's all!'

'Yes, so you keep saying!' Chad's hand snaked out and caught Bethany's wrist. 'Leave the clothes!' he ordered. 'I think we have a lot to talk about.' He sat up and tossed her dry things out of reach.

'Hey! What do you think you're doing?' Bethany cried. 'Let go of my wrist—you're hurting!'

'Be quiet!' Chad instructed tersely. 'Stop trying to tug free and you'll find my grip isn't at all painful. Now that's better!' He observed Bethany's rigid body, the taut, pale face for a moment in silence. 'Why do you keep running away from me, Bethany?' he asked quietly.

'I'm not...running away!' she replied unsteadily.

'It looks like it to me.'

'Well, maybe...maybe that's just the way your ego works!' she countered illogically. 'You're obviously so used to having women fall at your feet, maybe you can't handle it when...when...' She shook her head and looked away. 'Oh...oh, just forget it!' she added angrily, aware of Chad's mocking expression.

'You know, you sound as confused as you look.'

'Only because you make me that way!' Bethany retorted miserably. 'All I said was that I wanted to go back.'

Chad lifted his shoulders and smiled sardonically. 'As I said, running away.'

'Will you stop getting at me!' Bethany exploded, turning finally to look back into the strong, rugged planes of his face. 'I know you think I'm some sort of...of freak...an object of ridicule because I have resisted your...your dubious charms. But I don't happen to think it's such a crime to want to stick by my principles!' She glared at him, concentrating on trying to transform the smouldering tension into an inferno of anger, because that was the only way she knew how to handle it. 'Heaven knows, it's taken me long enough to focus on the good things,' she continued with breathless exasperation, 'to work out how I should live my life! I don't need——'

'And you think celibacy is a part of that?' Chad's dark brows screwed together in puzzlement.

'Why not?' Bethany swallowed, disconcerted by his frank appraisal of the situation. 'Of course,' she continued stiffly, 'I realise it's clearly a totally unfathomable concept for you! But then I don't happen to possess your casual attitude to certain things...'

Chad's jaw tightened, his eyes darkened dangerously, but miraculously his voice held the same conversational tone. 'Meaning?'

'You have a casual attitude to sex—you illustrated that very clearly only the other day!' Bethany responded shakily, remembering the humiliating scene with Theo on the staircase.

'It's a natural part of life,' Chad delivered bitingly. 'We don't all have hang-ups about it!'

Bethany swallowed convulsively. That hurt. God! Chad Alington was an unfeeling swine! If only he knew what she had been through! Anyone, *anyone* would feel the way she did now, wouldn't they?

She hesitated, half hoping for an apology that clearly was never going to come. 'Well, at least...at least I don't go around believing sex to be my God-given right!' Bethany declared. 'It's probably no more than a habit to you!' she added hurriedly, aware that she was skating on extremely thin ice. 'Well...well, I don't want to be part of your addiction! I am not another Theo!'

There was a strained silence, the only sounds the rhythmic crashing of the waves and the occasional barking of the dogs, who were playing in the surf. Bethany watched with trepidation as Chad inhaled a deep and controlling breath. What was she saying? How had she ever got into all this?

At last Chad spoke. 'If it weren't for the fact that we both know that what you've just said is an absolute load of total rubbish,' he murmured brutally, 'a smoke-screen of waffle to prevent you from facing up to the situation, to prevent you from facing up to yourself, then I might just find myself feeling a little annoyed. You? Another Theo?' His eyes raked her face in disbelief. 'Do I look that stupid?'

'Please! Let's forget it!' Bethany placed her free hand to her brow and released a taut breath. 'Look, you promised me a day on the beach with no...no hassle, remember?'

'So I'm a liar, as well as a sex maniac!' Chad replied sardonically. 'That surely doesn't surprise you!'

'Please, Chad! I really don't need any of this!' Bethany replied miserably.

'And you think I do?' His mouth curved into a derisive smile.

Bethany frowned. 'No...no, but——'

'You know...I know...what we both need!' His voice was rough-edged suddenly, a husky torment of sensuality that sent shivers running all over Bethany's body. He released her wrist and smoothed the flat of his hand along the line of her arm. 'Stop fighting it, Bethany!'

'Chad! Please! You promised!' Bethany's expression conveyed all of her anguish. Her heart was pounding like an express train running out of control. She ached with wanting him.

'Did I?' He seemed unconcerned.

'Yes!' She closed her eyes at his continued touch. 'You did!'

'Why is it so difficult for you to acknowledge what you feel?' he asked disbelievingly. 'Hell, Bethany, neither of us is made of stone! I can remember how it was in the cabin on that first occasion...can't you?'

She nodded briefly, opening her eyes to stare at the large brown hand that was tracing light feathery circles on her bare thigh.

'You know you wanted me then, just as much as I wanted you,' he pointed out firmly. 'If I had given into my instincts and persisted, worked at dissolving your inhibitions, maybe we wouldn't have both had to endure this long drawn-out and continued farce!' The superb bone-structure hardened as his other hand came up and tilted her face towards his. 'Bethany, are you listening to me?'

She shook her blonde head frantically. 'I...I don't know what you mean!'

'Oh, I think you do.' He moved closer, placing both hands at the small of her back, drawing her towards his body. 'You wanted me, Bethany—you still want me. I see it in every movement, every look. I can feel it in the air around you now. If I touch you...' He moved his hand and raised it to her trembling lips, a satisfied smile curving his firm mouth as Bethany shivered and closed her eyes. 'You see?'

'I don't want to see! Can't you understand that?' Bethany fixed him with a tremulous gaze. 'I'm not used to feeling like this!' she confessed shakily. 'I... I don't know how to handle it!'

'Let me help you then.' Chad's mouth moved against her lips. 'Don't be frightened, sweetheart,' he murmured huskily. 'I'm really not going to hurt you.'

Sweetheart! The endearment sounded wonderful. Bethany melted inside, became light-headed and unaware of her surroundings as Chad's hands traced a subtle pattern over her bare back, as he kissed her with a slow, lingering sexuality.

He raised his head after a long moment and smiled lazily. 'Better?'

Bethany raised her lashes and stared, trembling into the perceptive brown eyes. 'I'm not used... I mean... before I... he...'

Chad placed a finger to her lips. 'Shh! Forget the past. Just think of us...just think of now.' His mouth covered hers again, and this time the kiss was stronger and more persuasive, alive with erotic sensuality. He raised his head after a moment and looked into her eyes. 'Just relax,' he murmured. 'Concentrate on how good I make you feel.' His hands travelled to the towel that was still half draped around her and she felt it fall from her shoulders, registered dazedly his fingers, swift and effective, untying the bow at her neck.

'Chad!' She stiffened slightly, imploring him with deep green eyes. 'Please!' It was unclear whether she meant him to stop or go on; at any rate his fingers stilled a moment and his mouth slid down to cover hers again with sensuous command.

'I'm not going to hurt you ... Never, ever could I do that.' His voice was husky against the pale skin of her throat, slow and seductive as he allowed the ties of her bikini top to fall apart. Bethany shivered a little, felt the sweet, exquisite surge of sensation deep in the pit of her stomach, as his hands travelled slowly, oh, so slowly, to remove her damp top. 'You're beautiful, do you know that?' He smiled a devastating smile, pulling her close, sliding her with consummate ease so that she was effectively imprisoned by his strong muscular legs. 'I want you.'

Gently he laid her back on to the warm sand, his hands moving to mould her naked breasts with erotic ease, his gaze glittering with satisfaction as Bethany closed her eyes and gasped aloud.

She had never known such pleasure. Never imagined her body could come alive so quickly. 'Chad!' His name was a breath of delight on her lips as his mouth fell to each creamy mound in turn.

Her skin was on fire as she writhed and arched beneath his dominant figure. She felt his hands move lower, knew he could read her mind as his hands tugged away the remaining half of her bikini. His lips fell to the flat planes of her stomach, scorching the smooth skin with a trail of burning kisses. An infinitesimal pause, a slight movement, and then his mouth was covering hers again and she felt his naked length pressing against her.

For a brief moment she felt the old fear returning and she stiffened slightly, panicking a little as the solid contours of his body weighed down on her. 'It's all right, sweetheart.' He raised himself up and looked down into her face. 'It really is all right.'

It was. Bethany stared up into the deep, dark eyes and felt the ache in her body intensify as his hands stroked her inner thigh, moving gently to touch and tantalise her most sensitive place. 'I'm not going to hurt you.' His fingers stroked and explored every part of her as his mouth took lazy possession of her mouth.

On and on, his mastery knew no bounds as he brought Bethany to the brink of ecstasy. A moaning sound scorched the air between them; she gripped at his back, at his head, as wave after wave of sensation rippled through her body, gathering speed, intensifying with every heart-stopping second.

He made her wait, until wanting to feel him inside her was all she could think about. 'Chad, please!' This time there could be no doubt about the meaning of her cry. With a look of satisfaction, Chad raised himself above her and took possession with an exquisitely timed thrust. Then again, and again, until all meaning of time and place was blotted from Bethany's mind.

With an expertise that had her gasping aloud in the warm summer air, he continued to possess her, building up her need for him until she reached the summit of sensation, thrusting again, more powerfully this time, as her hands raked his back as she arched and writhed against him and was lost finally in a delirium of pleasure.

Bethany clasped her hands around Chad's neck after it was all over and held him close, burying her face in his neck, wanting the intensity, the contact, the unity to last forever. Chad, his breath coming in short, unsteady bursts, lay across her. She felt his mouth graze her skin, heard a few indistinct words that she prayed were other endearments.

'I never knew...' she whispered, shaking her head a little as she looked up into Chad's face. 'I never knew it could be like that.' She released a slow, steady breath, her expression one of wonderment and absolute disbelief.

She saw the attractive mouth smile lazily and felt a flare of pleasure as Chad bent his head and kissed her lips with slow sensuality. 'No, I guessed not. It took me an inordinate amount of time to work it out, but finally a few things became clear.'

'You called me sweetheart,' she murmured as his lips moved down to cover the tip of one naked breast.

'Is that so unusual?' He moved back and kissed her mouth again. 'You taste very sweet to me.'

'No one's...ever called me that before.'

'No?' He looked at her quizzically, then he smiled. 'Good. I'm pleased.' He rolled on to his side, trailing sensuous fingers across her full breasts, down over the flat planes of her stomach and beyond. 'Would you like a drink?' He reached behind for the cool box and produced a bottle of white wine and two long-stemmed glasses. 'It should really be champagne,' he declared silkily, 'but this will just have to do.' He sat up and undid the cork and then poured the chill, dry liquid into a glass, drank a little before handing it to Bethany. 'To my sweetheart,' he drawled huskily, dropping a kiss on to her mouth. 'Long may she continue to be fulfilled.'

She wanted to cry suddenly. It was ridiculous maybe, considering she had never felt so wonderful in all her life, but that was how emotion was—it sneaked up on you when you least expected it.

Bethany tipped the glass to her lips and finished the wine in one fell swoop, her wide green eyes consuming

Chad's face. I love him! The words tore at her heart as the truth finally hit her like a bolt from the blue. Not desire. Not just sex, but love!

Bethany shakily put down her glass and dragged her discarded towel around her shoulders. She loved Chad Alington. Heaven help her, it was true! She looked at him from beneath lowered lashes and felt the by now familiar stirring that was desire and love and need all mixed up in one.

He must never know, of course. She studied the magnificent bronzed body surreptitiously as he drank, and felt the first chill of realism sweep over her. He had fulfilled his task, completed what had surely been for him a typically male ambition—this first time sweetened, enlivened, because after all he had overcome at long last the barrier that she had persisted in erecting between them from the very first moment they had set eyes on one another.

Bethany swallowed against the tightness in her throat. That was all right—*it was*! After all, she had really and truly never expected anything else. He desired her. He had been—was being—gentle and kind. He had called her sweetheart. What else could she expect? She felt no shame, no regret. She loved him.

'Not cold, surely?' He was touching her again, dispelling all the doubts with a lazy investigation of her skin. 'Would you like some more wine?' He poured before she could answer, watched with amusement as Bethany downed the liquid in five seconds flat. Oh, no, she must never allow him to guess how deep her feelings ran—that would be too foolish and self-indulgent for words, and besides, it would end up with hurt and pain;

she couldn't risk that. Hadn't she endured enough of that to last a lifetime?

'If you're thirsty, Bethany, maybe you should stick with mineral water.'

'Sorry?' She concentrated on his words with effort. 'Oh, no, this is fine. I . . . I like the taste.'

Chad bent forward and took possession of her lips again. 'Mmm, tell me about it.'

He wanted her again. Bethany felt him stir against her and responded accordingly. She wanted him too. No shame. No doubt. It just felt right—absolutely right.

She parted her lips and accepted his hungry kiss. The wine had made her feel light-headed, daring too. She wrapped her arms around his neck, shrugging the towel from her shoulders, and pulled him closer, desperate for reassurance, thrusting her breasts against the solid contours of his chest, moving seductively against him as she stroked the bronzed skin, tangling her fingers in the mat of dark hair.

'Bethany, if I didn't know better,' Chad drawled as he took command of her wandering hands, 'I'd say you were trying to seduce me. Surely this is going from one extreme to another?'

She grinned wickedly. The wine had done wonders for her. 'Is there something wrong in that?'

He shook his head, an amused smile curving his lips. 'No. But I think . . .' His voice trailed away as she tipped her face towards his and kissed the firm, sensual mouth with hungry need. 'Mmm . . . Bethany . . . !' He pulled away a little and surveyed her with laughing eyes. 'You are one hell of a fast learner, do you know that?'

'Sorry.' She stiffened and drew back from his body. Chad had achieved his goal. She should have known it wouldn't, couldn't, be the same again.

'Hey, now what's this?' His voice had a warning edge. Chad tugged playfully at the long braid that reached halfway down her back. 'Don't start retreating from me again! I want you—of course I do, but there are other... considerations.'

'Such as?' Her voice was faint. Oh, God! Wasn't this just a polite way of rejecting her?

'Look at me.' He tugged her hair again and she turned slowly round. 'One of us has to be practical, and it looks as if it's going to have to be me. It may or may not have escaped your notice, sweet Bethany, but I didn't take any precautions just now.' He paused. 'Now, if I've misread the situation and you're... No, I thought not,' he murmured as Bethany looked dazedly into the handsome face and slowly shook her head. 'And I didn't, much to my annoyance, come prepared—so, despite what you may have thought, this seduction wasn't planned— hoped for, yes,' he added, running a finger across her brow, down her temple, along her cheek, until it came to rest on her full bottom lip. 'And I'm a responsible adult and perfectly healthy, so if that frown which has just appeared on your forehead, is due to worry over——'

'It's not!' Bethany looked away, and forced herself to relax. 'I... I think perhaps I should be getting dressed——'

Chad reached out and grasped her arm, forcibly turning her to face him. 'No more barriers, Bethany!' he warned. 'We've passed that stage, haven't we? Haven't we?' he persisted, when Bethany made no reply.

She nodded, taking a deep controlling breath, managing a shaky half-smile that clearly didn't do enough to convince.

'You're a very desirable woman,' Chad informed her roughly. 'Believe that. Believe in yourself, even if you don't believe in me.'

She forced another smile. Her throat ached with unshed tears. Everything had happened so fast: six months of married hell, eighteen months of lonely celibacy and now this...now Chad...It was wonderful and yet...it was also extremely frightening. She wasn't sure she knew how to cope.

'Could...you pass my clothes?' Her voice sounded surprisingly calm, almost normal. 'I'm starting to feel a little cold.' She stole a nervous glance as Chad reached across and retrieved her discarded shorts and top. 'Could I have some more wine?' she asked hesitantly, more as a way of distracting Chad's attention while she got herself dressed than for any other reason.

'Sure.' His mouth curled into a lazy smile. 'Just promise me you won't gulp it down in one go as you did a minute ago, that's all!'

Bethany dressed in ten seconds flat, not bothering with any underwear. It seemed kind of pointless now—after all, Chad had seen everything there was to see of her. He had been as intimate as any man had ever been...

Bethany closed her eyes and tried to blot out the vision of Philip, of all the degradation he had subjected her to. Why couldn't Chad have been the first?

'Are you OK?'

Bethany looked up, felt Chad's touch, saw his puzzled expression. 'Fine!' She worked harder at the charade of taking everything in her stride this time, accepted the brimming glass and took several good sips. 'Just . . . just a bit of a headache, that's all.'

'Maybe it would be a good idea to lay off the wine in that case,' Chad drawled, curling lean fingers around the glass and removing it from Bethany's grasp. 'Anyway,' he added teasingly, 'headaches are usually used as an excuse before the event—not after it!'

'I . . . I know,' Bethany muttered unsteadily, standing up. Philip had never tolerated such feeble excuses—not even in the beginning. 'Look, Chad, I really would like to get back now. I need some time . . . on . . . on my own,' she added quickly as Chad shrugged his shoulders in acquiescence.

'No way!' He pulled his shorts over the taut muscular thighs, every movement as smooth and fluid as Bethany had come to expect, and stood up, drawing her towards him. 'I've told you—no more running away!'

'But——'

'You've spent too long alone in that cabin, Bethany,' Chad cut in commandingly. 'We all need space, we all need to get away from time to time, but not to such a degree that——'

'I had no choice!' Bethany pressed her lips together and frowned. 'Don't you understand that!'

'Yes, yes, I know!' Chad assured her firmly. 'And in many ways I admire your spirit—turning unforeseen hardship and poverty into an ideal, a way of life, as you have is commendable, but——'

'It was necessary! A way of coping!' He didn't understand. He thought she was just another victim of the recession. Oh, if only he knew! Bethany hesitated, considered telling him everything—the truth, all the gory details of her marriage—but she paled at the prospect, felt faint at the thought of reliving the humiliation and, anyway, what would it achieve? She had spent the best part of two years trying to forget. 'I want to go back!' Her voice was weary, pleading, almost desperate as she looked into the angled face. 'Please, Chad!'

He looked at her in silence for a moment and then his hands dropped from her arms. 'OK, let's leave the beach. But there will be no Greta Garbo act. Understood?'

CHAPTER TEN

'WHERE are we going?'

Chad slanted Bethany a quizzical glance. The dogs had bounded up the track ahead of them, still full of energy. 'My place—where do you think?'

'But I should be getting back to the cabin!' Bethany halted uncertainly, her arm outstretched as Chad tugged her playfully.

'Not the cabin. Besides, you haven't finished your seduction routine yet!' His mouth curved teasingly. 'I'm looking forward to that. Maybe I'll allow you to go back later,' he added smoothly. '*Much* later!'

He dropped the holdall from his shoulder and pulled Bethany towards him, his eyes glittering with sudden animal vibrancy. 'I want you, Bethany Jones,' he whispered huskily, his lips moist and urgent against the soft skin of her throat. 'I want you very much.'

His hands roamed sensuously over her body, exploring and stroking with the touch of an expert. Immediately Bethany felt a quiver of pleasure lance through her, a stirring deep inside that signified the depth of her own needs and desires. She wound her arms around his neck, tangled her fingers through Chad's hair as his mouth slid across to cover hers, as his kiss deepened and his body hardened, knowing there was no way she could refuse him.

'Come on!' Chad's voice was unsteady and rough-edged as he reluctantly disentangled himself and tugged her determinedly up the track. They reached the side door, and he swung Bethany into his arms, carrying her over the threshold. The interior was refreshingly cool after the fierce August sunshine, but it did nothing to dispel the heat of expectation and desire that both of them were experiencing. Chad took the stairs two at a time, his bronzed muscles rippling powerfully as he shouldered open the door of the bedroom and carried Bethany across to the four-poster bed.

'Not here!' Bethany glanced at the carved wood and elegant hangings and shook her head wildly, clasping her fingers tightly around his neck, burying her face in his tanned shoulder to blot out the old visions. 'Please, Chad! Not here!'

'Why ever not?' He wasn't focusing on her words; his mind was clearly on other things as he kissed her throat, his mouth moist and urgent against her skin. 'Mmm, it's soft and cool and comfortable.' He laid her back on the bed, his large frame strong and masterful as he sat astride Bethany's slim body. 'Just right for what we had in mind!'

'Please!' Bethany stiffened and tried to pull away. 'You don't understand, Chad!' she whispered urgently as his lips moved to caress the tender skin of her throat. 'Please, I beg you!'

'Beg me?' His voice was husky with desire. He wasn't taking anything she said seriously. She saw the fleeting glimpse of his attractive mouth curve into a sensuous smile before he lifted her top and suckled the fullness of each breast. 'Mmm, I like the sound of that!' His hands travelled the length of her, coming to rest on the waistband of her shorts, slipping beneath the fabric, exploring the silken skin of her inner thigh...

Bethany stared up at the cream silk canopy overhead, her body tense with anguish. It had been glorious on the

beach, would have been wonderful anywhere else, but
not here, not in this room. It was too similar, the four-
poster too much like her old marital bed... For a moment
all she could see was Philip, all she could feel were *his*
rough, angry hands as they invaded her body and her
privacy.

'No!' It was a frantic cry. Bethany hit out wildly,
pummelling the bronzed back, pushing the dark head
away with frantic hands. 'Get away from me!' she cried
dazedly. 'Don't touch me!'

Chad stared into her pale, distraught face, his dark
gaze narrowing with puzzled incredulity, and then he
turned and rolled away, watching without a word as
Bethany scrambled from the bed and ran from the room
sobbing soundlessly.

'Ever heard of *déjà vu*?'

Bethany turned her head and gulped back the tears.
Chad was framed in the doorway, looking cool and controlled, watching her. 'I'm... I'm sorry!'

There was a short, sharp silence. 'And is that it?' Chad
enquired tersely. 'Is that all I get?'

She leaned back against the wall of the corridor and
tried to control her quivering features, conscious of
Chad's intense gaze. She was still breathing hard, still
upset, hardly able to believe that she had acted so aggressively. There was a jagged red scratch down his
temple where her nail had caught. She looked at it in
horror, 'I... I didn't mean to hit you.'

'No?'

Bethany screwed her eyes shut and shook her head,
hating the formidable chill in Chad's eyes. 'No.'

'So what, then?'

What could she say? Explain in a matter-of-fact voice
that somehow she had lost her grip on reality and had,

in that brief moment, been transported back to the days when, night after night, her husband had forced himself on to her, *raped* her? She cringed inwardly as the old feelings of humiliation swept over her. 'I ... I just don't feel comfortable with four-poster beds, that's all,' Bethany replied unsteadily, staring fixedly down at the floor.

He gave a harsh laugh. 'Well, that's novel! I'm expected to believe that pathetic explanation, am I? You slept in the damn thing without a word of complaint a few nights ago,' he reminded her evenly. 'Or had you forgotten?'

'No ...' Bethany shook her head. 'No, of course I hadn't.' She ran a shaky hand over her forehead and wished Chad would touch and hold her, instead of standing there with a foot of space between them, looking at her with that cold expression in his eyes. 'But then ... well, I was ill and ... and it was different.'

'You mean I wasn't forcing myself upon you?'

'Chad, please don't be like this!' she whispered, raising watery green eyes to his face.

'You mean totally confused?' Chad responded curtly. 'Because that's how I feel right at this moment! I thought we were over all this! You beat me away as if I was raping you in there!' he gritted. 'Your face held disgust and fear. How the hell do you expect me to be? More importantly, how do you expect me to *feel*?'

Not like this! Bethany screamed silently. Please, not like this! 'I know you think I'm ... I'm mad, but I'm not. I just can't explain, that's all ... maybe later——'

'Can't or won't?' He wasn't going to make it easy for her. 'Come on, Bethany! Tell me! Which is it?'

She stole an anguished glance at his face. 'I ... I don't know. Both, I suppose.'

'You don't sound very sure!'

'All right then, won't!' Bethany snapped tightly. 'Is that clear enough for you? I won't tell you!'

'You're already regretting it, aren't you?'

Bethany looked into the stunningly handsome face. 'What?' she whispered.

'Us making love! What the hell do you think I'm talking about?' he snarled.

For a brief second she considered his question seriously. If they hadn't made love this afternoon she wouldn't be standing here suffering now, wouldn't have to face that look of anger which tore at her heart and made her feel sick with anxiety. But regret that beautiful moment on the beach? No! How could she? She had felt numb before, an empty, hollow person, who didn't dare think or feel, someone going through the motions day after day, shutting down parts of herself because she couldn't bear to deal with all the old memories... And then Chad had come along. He was the first, the *only* man to make her come alive, to make her feel real and whole and *good*. So she was as scared as hell of this intense feeling, this love she felt for him, but she would work on that, work out how to deal with it in time... if she ever got the chance.

'It's OK! You don't need to answer!' Chad's brows had snapped together: she could feel the raw energy, the anger that emanated from him. 'I can read your expression well enough.'

'This is... is crazy, Chad!' Bethany's voice wobbled alarmingly as she looked into his face. 'Surely you don't imagine that what we... we did together on the beach——?'

'*Did* together?' Chad repeated harshly. 'God, you can't even phrase that decently!' He spun away, dragging a large hand through his hair in a gesture of frustrated anger. 'We made love, Bethany! Is it so difficult for you to say? And we were about to do the very same just now——!'

'I told you I didn't want to!' Bethany cut in desperately. 'I did! But you were carried away. You didn't want to listen! I tried to tell you about the bed——'

'Are you saying what I think you're saying?' Chad demanded savagely. 'Am I being accused of attempted *rape*?' He gave a harsh laugh of incredulity. 'Well, for your information, some of us aren't able to switch our feelings on and off like a tap!' he continued with cutting cruelty. 'Five seconds before and you were as desperate for sex as I was! Too blunt for you, Bethany?' he enquired, flicking dark angry eyes across her pale face. 'Well, maybe it's more of an honest description!' he growled. 'Clearly you're not happy with the "making love" tag! And the bed!' He shook his dark head. 'What the hell difference does that make?'

'It . . . it just does,' Bethany whispered.

'Well, explain, then!' Chad commanded. 'Tell me. I'm standing here listening!'

'I've already told you, I can't! I won't!' Bethany wailed.

At this moment, witnessing his anger, she doubted there would ever be a time when she would be able to. What would his reaction be if he ever knew the truth? She balled her hands into fists at her sides at the imagined scene. Disgust? Revulsion? She might as well kill this thing off right now, before it got anywhere. It would only bring her heartache and pain in the end. Why prolong the suffering? 'Anyway,' she continued wildly, 'I can see from your expression that it would do no good! You're angry because I've dented your macho image.

You thought that after the beach everything would be a foregone conclusion, didn't you? Well, it's not like that! *I'm* not like that!'

Dark eyes narrowed, contemplating her wild face with a mystified expression. 'How can you say that?'

'Oh, don't look at me like that!' Bethany snapped. 'You think I'm a total innocent? You think I don't know how men's minds work?'

She thought of her marriage to Philip, what he had put her through, the things he had forced her to see and do, and closed her eyes tight shut. It hadn't been her fault; she had been young and innocent, totally in awe of him... frightened... desperately frightened. But she should have left him sooner. She should have made the break after that first horrific night. But she had had no one to turn to... Where would she have gone...?

Feeble excuses! She knew it. Chad would know it too! The truth was, she should never have allowed Philip to treat her the way he did.

'I see!' His deep voice was clipped. She opened her eyes and saw the lines of grim disapproval, the cold, mechanical expression. 'It seems I've over-estimated. I thought maybe we had reached a stage where you could place a little trust in me.' His voice hardened. He lanced her with a look that hurt. 'Obviously I was wrong.'

'It seems we've both made a big mistake!' Bethany cried, anguish etched all over her face.

'How right you are!' His eyes were as cold and as hard as ice as they scoured her face. 'You said before that you wanted to be on your own—well, now it's my turn. I'll give you a lift back to the cabin if you wish——'

'No!' Pride made Bethany's voice keep level. She took a breath and forced a modicum of control into her expression. 'No...no, thank you. I'll walk back.'

'Fine.'

His indifference was like a knife twisting in her heart. She wanted to cry and sob aloud. She wanted to tell him how she really felt, how difficult it was for her to trust and hope. She wanted to tell him how much she *loved* him.

Stiffly, her throat aching with unshed tears, Bethany moved to the top of the stairs.

'Bethany...!' She turned and glanced at the powerful profile, her heart leaping a little in desperation. 'Nothing.' Chad's voice was hard. He turned and walked back into the bedroom. 'Forget it,' he said, closing the door behind him. 'Just forget it!'

Time passed slowly, oh, so slowly. A day felt like a week, a week more like a month. Bethany felt as if she were suffering in slow motion.

She considered many things in that time, one of them being the possibility of packing up and moving away. After all, hadn't wealthy, generous Philip left her everything? She had the money. She didn't need to live like this. But the thought of not seeing Chad ever again... She wasn't sure if she could bear that. At least living here, so close, meant there was the chance of a meeting, a chance of reconciliation.

Chad obviously didn't feel the same way. Bethany was in her truck, returning from a rare trip into town, when she saw the "For Sale" signs being erected. She felt as if she had been forcibly struck, so great was the shock. It was as though the world had fallen away from beneath her feet and she had nothing to grasp on to.

She brought the vehicle to a shaky standstill and stared and stared at the red and white signs, and felt misery welling up inside her like a sickness. Chad was leaving? Oh, God! Please don't let him go! Please! The thoughts screamed through her head at one hundred miles an hour. If he left, she didn't know what she would do. He had to be near! He had to!

Bethany turned off the engine and got out of the truck. Her heart was thudding wildly as she took a few tentative steps towards the heavy front door. He was in— or at least his car was parked outside. It didn't necessarily follow that he was at home—he could have taken himself off for a long walk somewhere...

She had just plucked up enough courage to lift the rounded iron knocker when the door opened suddenly and Chad appeared. He looked as magnificent as ever dressed in an immaculate dark grey suit, a crisp fine-lined grey and white shirt with a burgundy silk tie perfectly knotted at the neck. He was obviously off somewhere on business. Perhaps, Bethany thought miserably, he was off to do a deal with his banker, perhaps he had already found another home...

'Hello.'

Bethany flushed, heat running through her limbs like fire at the sound of his deep, controlled tones.

'You're leaving.' The statement of fact had passed her lips before she could stop it.

Chad glanced across at the red and white board displayed prominently at the end of the drive. 'Looks like it.'

Bethany swallowed and forced her expression to remain neutral. 'Soon?'

Chad raised dark brows. 'Who knows? The property market isn't particularly easy to judge. And as you can see,' he continued, 'the boards have only just gone up.'

'I...I thought you liked it here,' Bethany murmured. 'I mean, I'm amazed you should spend so much money doing the place up,' she added in harder tones, 'and then sell it so soon after.'

'The amount I've invested is reflected in the asking price,' Chad informed her laconically. 'Don't worry, Bethany,' he added softly, focusing steadily on her face. 'I'm an excellent businessman. I've made sure that I won't lose any money.'

He was so distant, so controlled. Bethany swallowed and licked at her suddenly parched lips. There were hundreds of things she wanted to say, but for some reason every word, every thought, tied itself into a knot in her brain. She had gone over all that had happened between them so many times, and yet now she was here...

'Chad, I really would like to speak to——'

'Ready to go?' Theo. A startling impression of wild, dark hair, designer labels and exotic perfume glided through the open door, hitting Bethany for six. 'Oh, it's you.' She glanced down at Bethany disdainfully and then linked her arm proprietorially through Chad's. 'We're just on our way out, so if you're...selling something, or——'

'Cut it out, Theo!' Chad's voice was sharp. 'Bethany was passing, she happened to see the signs, that's all.'

The blood-red mouth widened into a malicious smile. 'Not interested in buying the place, by any chance?' she enquired tauntingly. 'But then, it's just a teensy, weensy bit out of your price-range, I should imagine! Still, you carry on selling your stuff at market, or whatever it is you do, and you never know, you might just be able to afford it one day!'

Chad lifted Theo's arm from his, like a limpet being prised from a rock. 'Go and wait in the car, will you? I'll be over in a minute.'

She frowned. 'We'll be late for the first race.'

'No, we won't! Now go! You've got a smear of lipstick on your teeth,' he informed her carelessly. 'You can spend the time seeing to that.'

Chad waited until the sound of Theo's high heels had died away, then he looked down at Bethany. 'You were saying?'

'Nothing, it...it doesn't matter.' She felt she might be sick any minute. The tension was unbearable. She had been so close to making a fool of herself...so desperately close...

'It looks as if it does.' Chad had caught hold of her arm before she could turn away. 'It looks as if it matters very much indeed.'

'I...I was just curious about the signs.' Bethany inhaled a steadying breath. 'Would you mind letting go of my arm, please.'

'Theo has very bad timing, doesn't she?' Chad murmured grimly. 'I'm sorry about that.'

'Oh, yes, I'm sure you are!' Her mouth curled into a smile that held no trace of amusement. 'How could you?' she added, her voice dripping with disgust.

'How could I what?' Chad's dark brows snapped together.

Bethany struggled hard to hold on to her composure. 'You know very well what I'm talking about!' she croaked. 'Don't tell me I'm reading the situation wrongly, because I won't believe a word!'

'Are you referring to the fact that you think I slept with Theo?' Chad's dark eyes sparked anger.

'I *think* you slept with Theo?' Bethany shook her head. 'What do you take me for—a complete fool? I don't think, I know!'

'It clearly matters, at any rate,' Chad responded smoothly. 'The idea that I should share my bed with someone else so soon after making love to you—now why is that, I wonder?' His mouth curved into a provocative smile. 'Care to explain it all for me, Bethany?'

'You're an arrogant swine!' she hissed, jerking her arm free.

The broad shoulders lifted in a shrug. 'Tell me something I don't know! I am what I am. You should know that much by now.'

'I never thought you'd do this! I never thought you'd *leave*!' She felt herself begin to crumble under the uncompromising gaze. It was clear he didn't care; she had been right not to hope, not to believe in fairy-tale endings.

She turned and ran towards the truck, opened the driver's door, slammed it shut and sped away down the track towards the cabin, driving through a mist of tears.

The idea of actually buying Chad's home occurred to Bethany later that same night. Theo's sarcastic few words had come back to her out of the blue, striking a chord of defiance which shocked and startled her.

Bethany shook her head in disgust as she paced back and forth in the cabin, working herself up into a maelstrom of emotion, going over and over everything in her mind. The vision of the two of them in bed together tormented her over and over again.

Bethany glanced around at her simple home and knew that it was time for this part of her life to change. This place had been good for her, it had saved her sanity, but all of a sudden she felt quite claustrophobic, as if the walls were just a little too near, a little too restrictive.

Yes. It was time for a change. Not a total metamorphosis: she would still keep her hens and her goats, still live a comparatively frugal life, but she was young and life was passing her by and she had all this money sitting in the bank doing nothing. She had given hundreds of thousands away to charity and still it sat there, building up interest month after month, reminding her. Maybe she should have got rid of every last penny—often that had been the temptation. But she was only human, and the thought of poverty, *real* poverty, frightened her just like everyone else.

Bethany took a deep breath. Yes. It was the right decision. A good way to use the last of Philip's inheritance. Perhaps she could do something useful with the house—a holiday home for deprived children perhaps? Yes! Yes, why not? Her face brightened at the thought. It would be something she could lose herself in...a way of forgetting...

Whatever happened, she couldn't continue to stay here, dwelling on things that might have been. She took a determined breath and released it slowly. Chad Alington didn't love her—she would have to face that fact and live with it. She still had some pride. She wouldn't just let him walk out of her life without some sort of show of strength.

The time had come to prove she wasn't afraid of living any more.

CHAPTER ELEVEN

'Now this is the dining-room. A lovely aspect as you can see, and so perfectly proportioned. Renovated beautifully, and with a great deal of thought too. The two sets of French windows open out on to this newly designed terrace. Look at that view! Magnificent, isn't it?'

The short bald-headed man turned and beamed, looking for reaction. Bethany smiled a little as silence fell in the high-ceilinged room. The estate agent hadn't stopped talking since he'd escorted Bethany out of his car and guided her eagerly towards the front door. He was certainly giving it his all, but then that wasn't surprising, she thought vaguely. The asking price was near half a million pounds and his firm's percentage would be substantial.

It was weird being shown around Chad's home. It was depressing her more than she had anticipated. He wasn't here, of course. She had made doubly sure that the estate agent was aware of her aversion to viewing a property when the owner was present before she had made the appointment. She was in disguise. She had shown the efficient little man with his bald head and briefcase proof of her ability to purchase, and all the noughts on her bank statement had been enough to secure the VIP treatment. Her plan had been carried out with the sort of precision planning that was almost military—maybe Chad would have been impressed.

Bethany glanced in the large ornate mirror that hung over the Adam fireplace. To be taken seriously she had had to change her image, of course—and she was serious about all this—*deadly* serious. For the first time in a long while she was dressed with emphasis on quality and flair, styling and colour. Her cream linen suit and beige leather sandals had been bought with care, as had the simple but tasteful additions: a silk scarf draped casually around her neck, some jewellery—discreet gold earrings and one large bangle around her slender wrist. Bethany had taken the time to draw her honey-coloured hair into a soft chignon to frame her face, had even taken the trouble to emphasise her English-rose features with a little neutral eyeshadow and carefully applied lipstick.

'I'm sure you'll agree this house certainly is a bargain, Miss Jones!' The estate agent was off once again. 'This calibre of property doesn't come on to the market that often—not at such a competitive price anyway. The owner is after a quick sale. Wants everything sewn up before he goes out to Australia——'

'Australia?' Bethany stopped in her tracks. She had wandered out through the French windows on to the terrace; now she turned sharply and fixed the small man with a wide green-eyed stare of disbelief. 'Did you say Australia?'

'Yes, indeed.' The agent clasped pudgy hands together in a cheerfully brisk manner. 'Beautiful country, so I'm told. Although even out there you'd be hard pushed to find something as spectacular as this view. Just look at that, Miss Jones!' he delivered earnestly, waving his arms in a wide arc. 'Have you ever seen anything so magnificent?'

Bethany followed his gaze. It was a perfect summer day and the vast expanse of the English Channel reflected the rich deep blue of the sky. The lush green of the Devon coastline rose and fell spectacularly away in both directions... Yes, it was glorious, she thought fervently. So how was it Chad could think about leaving this place? And not only this county but this country too. Australia—the other side of the world... Did he dislike her *that* much?

She shook her head in exasperation, chiding herself the instant the thought had entered her head. Too melodramatic, too self-indulgent for words! What made her think she was the reason for Chad selling up and moving away? But *Australia*? Bethany heaved a despondent sigh. And then she remembered a previous conversation. He had a sister out there, didn't he? Surely Chad was just going to visit?

'Is... is the owner staying out in Australia, do you know?' Bethany worked hard at keeping the emotion from her voice. 'I mean, is it a permanent move?'

'As far as I know,' came the cheerful reply. 'Mr Alington did refer to a new life—that sort of thing. Now, shall we meander back inside? You haven't seen the upstairs rooms yet. There are nine bedrooms, three with *en-suite* facilities. Decoration work hasn't started on most of these rooms, although of course structurally they've been made perfectly sound... Miss Jones?' The gushing had stopped. Bethany turned her head and saw through misted eyes that the estate agent was looking at her with some puzzlement. 'Ready to view the rest of the house?'

'No.' She swallowed and took a controlling breath. 'No, it's all right, Mr... er, Mr Chalmers. I've seen all I want to see. I want to buy it... for the asking price.'

The large expanse of forehead creased into a frown. 'But you've only seen a fragment of the house! Surely you'd like to see the——'

'No!' Bethany's reply was sharper than she intended. With a great deal of effort she softened her voice, changed her expression to one of pleasure. 'This really is the place I've been looking for, I can assure you of that.' She glanced with unseeing eyes at her watch and played the part of a busy working woman. 'You see, I'm under rather a tight schedule today——'

'Of course! Of course! I understand, Miss Jones. Do forgive me!' The little man's smile was conciliatory as he waited for Bethany to re-enter through the French windows. 'Well, the owner will be pleased!' He beamed. 'I promised him our firm would come up with a quick sale and you can't get quicker than this, can you? You have no property to sell, I understand, Miss Jones, and are keen to move in as soon as possible?'

'What?' Bethany frowned, forcing herself to focus for just a little longer on her companion's words. 'Oh...oh, yes. It will be a cash purchase.' She smoothed back a stray strand of hair from her face, glad of the cool interior. 'That shouldn't take too long, should it?'

'No, no indeed! You should be able to move in at the end of next month if all goes smoothly.'

Roughly six weeks and she would be living here. It was an unbelievable thought. Was she really doing the right thing? Bethany wondered, glancing round the room in a daze. She had acted so quickly, so impulsively, setting her plans into motion like a woman possessed.

The estate agent, with continued efficiency, tidied away his papers, snapped his briefcase shut and walked out into the hall.

Bethany fiddled nervously with the scarf at her neck. Was this *really* a good idea?

'Ah, Mr Alington, you're back!'

Her fingers gripped tightly at the swirl of floral silk around her throat for an instant. *Chad? Here? Now?* Her heart thumped violently at the prospect of coming face to face with him, leaped again as she heard the familiar sound of his measured footsteps crossing the tiled hallway.

'Congratulations, Mr Alington! You have a buyer! I was only just saying that this should be one of the quickest purchases on record!'

Quickly Bethany dodged around the long polished table, glad for once of Mr Chalmers' effusive chatter, which would surely give her the chance she needed to escape.

'Indeed?' Chad didn't sound particularly interested.

'Yes! Miss Jones was so taken with the view that she didn't even need to——'

'Miss Jones?' The footsteps had halted.

'Yes, that's right!' The estate agent latched on to the sudden interest in his client's voice. 'Beautiful young woman—I'll introduce you, shall I?'

Bethany scurried over to the now closed French windows and turned the handle expectantly. She would be able to dodge through the hedge and run down the track without either of the men being any the wiser. Later she would phone up the estate agent and make her apologies, but for now the most important thing was that Chad shouldn't see her, shouldn't realise exactly who the purchaser of his house really was.

The doors wouldn't budge. Bethany moved frantically to the other set and cursed silently as they too refused to open. Damn the efficient Mr Chalmers! What the hell had he locked them for? She scanned the room for another way out, acutely conscious that Chad and the estate agent were only just outside the dining-room door.

'Miss Jones. May I introduce the owner, Mr Alington?'

She had considered hiding behind the long, thick drapes at the window—anything to escape from that dark, piercing gaze. Instead she turned as Chad entered the room, keeping her gaze fixed on the magnificent view, praying that somehow, something would happen, so that she wouldn't have to endure this confrontation.

She didn't turn around immediately. Five full seconds passed.

The estate agent cleared his throat and tried again. 'Er...Miss Jones, the owner's called by unexpectedly. I hope you don't mind if——'

'*Bethany*?' Chad's eyes narrowed in disbelief as she finally turned. She moved forward and gripped the back of one of the dining-chairs for support, aware of the amazement on his face, the astonishment in his eyes.

Bethany gazed into the tanned, incredibly handsome face and gulped a quick breath. 'Hello, Chad.' He looked his usual dark and dynamic self. Her eyes registered a smart, perfectly tailored suit, car keys and dark sunglasses held in one large hand, a sheaf of papers gripped tightly in the other.

'Ah! You know each other! What a small world it——!' The estate agent began.

'What are you doing here?' Chad's eyes narrowed. She saw his gaze sweep her figure, the dark eyes digesting her designer outfit in an instant. 'Is this some kind of foolish joke?'

'No... Why should it be?' Her voice wasn't as strong as she had hoped. She tried to look defiant, although instinct told her she hadn't succeeded.

'Because you're here, in my house, dressed like that!' Chad shot back. 'Why do you think?'

The effusive estate agent had fallen into uncomfortable silence. Now he plucked up courage, his pudgy face creased into lines of confusion as he attempted to take on the role of mediator. 'Is...is there some problem here?'

'Would you leave us?' Chad's voice was curt. 'Miss Jones and I have a few things we wish to discuss.'

'No!' Bethany dragged her eyes away from Chad's face and implored the small man with wide green eyes. 'No! Please——'

'Get out of my house now!' Chad didn't even glance in his direction. The command was absolute—there was no way anyone in his right mind would disobey.

Bethany watched the estate agent scurry out of the room, heard his hesitant, mumbled assurance that he would be waiting outside in the car, should he be needed. 'You didn't have to be so rude!' she delivered flatly. 'The man was only doing his job!'

'Forget him! I want to know what the hell all this is about!' Chad demanded grimly. 'Have you finally flipped, or what?'

Bethany inhaled deeply; several uneven breaths that didn't do her a bit of good. 'And why should I have done that?' she inquired stiffly.

'Oh, no reason at all!' Chad thundered sarcastically. 'I mean, what could be more obvious than to find you here, fooling that idiot of a man into believing you can buy this place, looking as if you've just stepped out of the fashion pages of some glossy magazine——!'

'You think I'm mad, don't you?' Bethany cut in harshly.

'What the hell am I supposed to think?' Chad responded grimly. He shook his head and cast blazing eyes over the cream linen suit. 'Look at yourself! I'm no expert, but even I can see that you must have spent a fortune on that outfit.'

'Don't you like it?' Why had she asked that? Why?

'Like it? You look gorgeous! But what's that got to do with anything?' Chad demanded. 'I want to know why you've chosen to waste—what was it?—four, five hundred pounds on——'

'It's none of your business how much my outfit cost!' Bethany snapped. 'I had to have it—do you really think the estate agent would have taken me seriously in my tatty dungarees and wellies? He'd have taken one look and laughed in my face!'

Chad shook his head in disbelieving exasperation. 'You've put yourself in debt! And for what? Just to play some foolish game? Never mind the estate agent! Is it any wonder *I* think you're mad?'

'You're going to Australia.' Bethany's voice was flat. She stared down at her feet. 'Why?'

'Why not?' His retort was terse; clearly he wasn't in the mood to be helpful.

'But…it's so far. Are you going out to visit your sister? Is that it?'

'I'll see her while I'm there, no doubt. But that's not the main reason.' Bethany looked up and waited for him to continue. Chad's expression, as usual, didn't tell her a thing. 'I've decided on a change of continent,' he continued jerkily, reluctantly almost. 'It's a good place for solitude.'

'I see.'

'Do you?' Chad's eyes scoured her face. 'I doubt that!'

'The estate agent told me you hoped to have everything settled before you left,' Bethany murmured. 'I don't think he could believe his luck when I told him I had no house to sell, that I too hoped for a quick purchase.'

'Bethany! Will you listen to what you're saying?' The sheaf of papers was unceremoniously dumped on the polished mahogany dining-table, the car keys and sunglasses clattering after them. Chad moved around the table and gripped her by the shoulders, pulling her towards the French windows so that the light was full on her face. 'Stop this pretence now! It's pointless, can't you see that?'

'There is no pretence.' Her voice was low, full of emotion. It was agony having him so close, touching her like this, and yet knowing she didn't have him at all—would never have him.

'Do you honestly believe I *want* to go to Australia?' he demanded roughly. He gave her shoulders a rough shake. 'Well, do you?'

'You're going, aren't you?' Bethany replied quietly. 'You've put this place up for sale.'

'Yes!' Chad released his grip and inhaled a deep breath, glancing out at the sea. 'Yes, I have...' He paused and his eyes flicked to Bethany's rigid face. 'I had an offer from an Australian journal to write a few articles,' he continued, half to himself. 'An unexpected avenue that seemed like a sign. Over the years I've nurtured a fatalistic attitude to life.' He shrugged, as if casually, but there was a tension in the broad shoulders, a rigidity in the movement. 'This Australian offer seemed too big a twist of fate to ignore——'

'Well, I'm pleased for you!' Bethany cut in, unable to bear their stilted conversation a moment longer. 'Now, if you'll excuse me...!' She turned away and half ran around the table towards the door of the dining-room. She couldn't cope with any more of this. Much longer and she'd break down completely in front of Chad...

'Bethany! Not so fast!' There was no escape; he was quicker than she, blocking the only exit with his broad, rugged frame. They stared at one another in silence for a moment, then Chad asked with rough-edged persistence, 'I want you to tell me what you thought you would achieve by coming here today. I really want to understand why you arranged this pointless meeting with the estate agent.'

Bethany looked up into the dark eyes and took a deep breath. 'It wasn't a pointless meeting, Chad,' she murmured shakily. 'I'm... I'm not mad, whatever you may think. I've made up my mind to buy this place. Besides...' She swallowed and tried to inject a note of lightness into her voice. 'Besides, someone else might turn the dear old prison into a hotel or something—I couldn't bear that.'

'No, they wouldn't.' His deep voice was quiet, without emphasis. 'I've put that down as a condition of purchase: no businesses run from here, no hotels. I'm surprised the efficient Mr Chalmers hadn't got round to telling you that. I've even had a clause added whereby you are allowed the continued use of the beach.'

'You have?' Bethany looked into the handsome face and didn't bother to hide her amazement. She shook her head. 'That...that was very generous of you. But I don't understand. Why?'

Chad shook his head, his mouth twisted into a dry, attractive smile that sent her heart leaping against her chest. 'You love the beach—I didn't want to deprive you of that.' Dark, smouldering eyes pierced hers for a moment.

Bethany frowned. She wanted so much to tell him how she felt. The burden of keeping her love for him a secret was weighing so heavily.

'So, tell me,' he continued briskly, after the brief pause had lengthened into a tense and smouldering silence, 'where are you planning to get half a million pounds from? Do you rob banks in your spare time, is that it?' His voice had started out calm; now it was unsteady and a little rough-edged.

'Don't joke!' Bethany closed her eyes for a second in despair. 'There... there are things...' she began, in a voice that was noticeably shaky now, '...things I haven't told you, Chad...'

Dark brows drew together in a frown. 'Such as?'

Bethany pressed her lips together to stop them trembling, swallowed, hesitated some more and finally spoke. 'I...I was married. My...my husband died. It was a heart attack. He left me everything.' Bethany paused and looked into the taut, dark features. No expression. No hint of how he was taking the unexpected information. She cleared her throat nervously and forced herself to continue. 'I...I gave a lot of the money away after he died, but even so, I'm still a very wealthy woman...too wealthy.'

There was a long, long silence. Bethany half wondered if Chad had heard what she'd said. She risked another glance into his face and flinched at what she saw there—clearly he had.

'I see.' Chad's gaze was unflinching. 'How long ago did this happy union take place?'

'Almost two years.'

'How long before he died?'

'Chad, please!'

'How long?' His face was a mask: a grim, hard, cold mask.

'A little under six months.'

'And did you love him?'

Bethany ran a shaky hand over her brow. 'Before . . . I don't know . . . I imagined I did. But later——'

'And am I expected to murmur the usual words of condolence?' Chad cut in harshly. 'Is that what you want?'

Bethany licked at her dry lips and shook her head a fraction. 'No! No, of course it's not!' she replied frantically. 'To be honest——'

'Honest?' Chad's lips curled in derision. 'Are you sure you know the meaning of the word?' He leaned back against the door and let out a fierce expletive, dragging a large hand through his sleek, dark hair. 'I don't believe this!' he murmured, shaking his head. 'I don't believe you're doing this to me!' He fastened his gaze back on Bethany's face. 'So why the shack? Why the pretence at poverty? Why the *lies*?'

His intense scrutiny unnerved her. Bethany looked away, only to find her chin tilted back towards the formidable face with strong, insistent fingers.

'Tell me, Bethany!' he demanded savagely.

'I haven't told you any lies!' Bethany replied helplessly. 'I haven't!'

'Well, there sure as hell was precious little truth flowing from your direction!' Chad retorted with cutting emphasis. 'I fell hook, line and sinker for the whole charade, didn't I?' he continued. 'Me!' He gave a harsh laugh. 'The hard man who prides himself on his cynicism. The fool who was under the illusion that maybe, just maybe, there was a chance of finding some real happiness with a girl who he thought was pure and innocent and *different*!' He threw her a scathing look. 'Well, this is different, I suppose, but it's not what I had in mind!' He shook his head and released a taut breath. 'Not at all!'

'Chad! What are you saying?'

'I'm saying I'm a fool, that's what I'm saying! There were parts of you that were a mystery to me; I accepted that. But through all the puzzlement, through all the confusion, I consoled myself with the fact that you were an honest girl who lived by standards that were on another plane from the rest of us mere mortals. I maybe didn't understand what was going on in that head of yours half the time, but I valued your integrity, your honesty! Ha!' He released a short, harsh laugh. 'Pretty stupid of me, eh? Now of course it all makes sense: you were like a crab, retreating back into your shell, scuttling away to the safety of your crumbling holiday home when things got a bit tricky between us!' He glared at her. 'My God! What an interesting challenge it must have been for you! Living the life of a pauper for a few weeks of the year, stringing me along! The poor little rich girl! The wealthy widow Bethany!'

'Chad, it wasn't like that!' Bethany implored, hating the way he was paralysing her mind by the sheer force of his anger. 'I wasn't trying to deceive you. The cabin really is my home——'

'Well, would you mind telling me why? What the point of the whole charade was, then?' he demanded roughly. 'Because I sure as hell can't fathom any of it out!'

'Will it make any difference?' Bethany asked dazedly. 'Will it make you any less angry with me?'

Smouldering dark eyes bit into her. 'Probably not. But I've always been a stickler for tying up loose ends.

I may as well hear your explanation—if you have one, that is!'

'Don't look at me like that!' Bethany pleaded. 'You're standing there . . . with that expression on your . . . your face . . . looking at me as if . . .'

'As if what?'

'You really hate me!' Bethany spun away and retreated back into the room.

'*Hate* you?' Chad's tone held incredulity. 'Do you honestly think I'd be this uptight about everything if I *hated* you?'

'I don't know!' Bethany wailed. 'All I know is I can't go on like this! I've existed in an emotional vacuum for nearly all of my life.' She turned, scrubbing a hand across her tear-stained cheeks. 'It won't make any difference to you—I honestly don't expect anything from you—but I must make you understand how this has happened. How I *feel*!'

'Bethany——'

'No, Chad!' She shook her head violently. 'Let me finish, please! Just let me say this much and then you can forget I ever ranted and raved like this!' She stumbled over to a chair and dragged it out, hiding her face in her hands for a minute, trying desperately to put her thoughts into some kind of order. 'I married when I was eighteen.' She pressed her hands to her cheeks and fought to make her voice sound calm. 'He was a lot older than me. I was too young, emotionally far younger than others of my age. My . . . my mother died when I was small. I was passed along a succession of elderly relatives. No one wanted me and you couldn't blame them really . . .' She took a shaky breath. 'Sounds ridiculous maybe, but I met my husband at a horse trial—I was in the St John Ambulance brigade, you see. He . . . he fell off his horse and fractured his wrist...' She looked across at Chad, saw the grim expression, the clenched bone-structure. 'It was a whirlwind affair.' She shook her head a little and frowned. 'For some reason he seemed to find me attractive. He swept me off my feet. I felt like a princess. I had never had attention like it before. He was suave, sophisticated, more worldly-wise... incredibly wealthy. After only a few weeks he asked me to marry him.'

'Bethany, what is the point of all this?' Chad strode across the room to the French windows. 'I sure as hell don't want to hear it, and besides, it's obviously painful for you. You loved him...' Chad's voice hardened a little. 'Still love him——'

'No!' She scraped the chair back suddenly and stood up. 'Don't say that! Never, never say that! He was a monster! A cruel, hateful man who made my life a misery!'

'*What*?' Chad spun around and faced Bethany, his eyes no longer cool, his expression no longer detached.

Bethany summoned up all of her strength and continued, her voice becoming harder as the memories became more painful. 'He drank. I had no idea what he was really like...' She bit down on her bottom lip. 'I was a virgin when we met. Totally unaware of... of the realities of life. I had this rosy image, you see... I had been living out fantasies in my mind that didn't exist.' She closed her eyes. 'He shattered all that on our wedding-night. He was drunk, uncaring...' She gulped and paused. 'I was petrified. I prayed things would improve, but they only got worse. He became more and more demanding, more violent...'

'He hit you?'

Bethany nodded. 'He became a different person once we were married. I was his possession, he said. He clothed and fed me and gave me beautiful things, and in return I was nothing more than his...his legal whore.'

'Bethany!' agonised eyes held her tormented face. 'Don't say any more.'

'I know I must disgust you.' Bethany lowered her head. Her fingers clenched convulsively around the flimsy fabric of her scarf. 'I disgust myself. I put up with...with his degradation for six months: hiding from him, hoping things would change, feeling for long periods that maybe I was to blame, that somehow it was my fault he treated me as he did. I should have left.'

'Why...didn't you?'

Bethany frowned at the stilted question. 'I've asked myself that question over and over. I did think of it. I did almost try it once, but he had forbidden me contact with any of my old friends and they wouldn't have wanted to know me, and besides what would I have told them? I was so ashamed.'

'No one knew?'

'Oh, no!' Bethany shook her head. 'That was what made it so...so difficult. He was such a charming man. Liked by everyone. And powerful, well thought of—he kept the company of cabinet ministers and lords. I would have had no chance of convincing anyone of how things really were—it would have been my word against his.'

'And then the bastard died.'

Bethany looked into Chad's taut face. He looked savage, fierce, as if he would like to kill someone.

'Yes. He hadn't written a will. As next of kin I got everything.'

'You've never told this to anyone before?'

'N-no. I ran away from everything, everyone. For several weeks I stayed in hotel rooms, hating every minute of it, trying to work out what I should do. Then I moved out of London and came to the coast. I had an idea the sea air would do me good. It did.'

'You found the cabin?'

'Yes. It was even more run-down than it appears now. I found out who owned it. Bought it from a local farmer who had almost forgotten it was there and... and began to work at healing myself.'

'And you were doing fine, until I came along and opened up all the old wounds.' His voice was flat.

Bethany nodded. 'S-something like that—although the healing part... I'm not sure that's true. All I had succeeded in doing was blocking out that part of my life. Forcing myself to forget all the shame and the anger instead of facing up to it... learning to deal with it.'

'I'm sorry. I'm so very, very sorry.' There was a desperate, heart-wrenching intensity in his voice.

Bethany watched uncertainly as Chad moved towards her. 'Chad, I... I just need to say something else.' She took a deep breath, saw the already tense body halt and stiffen. 'You probably think I'm an emotional wreck, you probably think I'm unstable, but I'm not. I feel real again... whole.' Her brow indented. 'And it's all because of you. I couldn't handle my feelings at first, but now I can. I know it's too late, but... but I have to tell you.'

'Let me say it first.' Chad moved slowly and carefully towards her, his eyes never leaving her face. He took her by the hand and raised her fingers to his lips. 'I love you, Bethany.' Strong, tanned fingers gently caressed her face. 'I need you. I want you. I love you.' His voice was deep, gruff with intense emotion. He smoothed back the strands of golden hair from her misted eyes and kissed a tear-drop as it fell on to her cheek. 'You are so fragile, Bethany Jones. In so much need of love... *my* love.' His mouth dropped to her quivering lips and he kissed her with a slow, lingering passion. 'I want to take care of you always,' he added softly. 'I will never, *ever* hurt you.'

'You . . . you really love me? You don't care about the past? About *my* past?' Bethany whispered unsteadily.

'There is no past. Only now, only the future.' Chad pulled her closer against his strong masculine body. 'I was a fool before—trying to take your rejection in my stride, trying to pretend it didn't matter, when in reality it hurt like hell. I think it was then that I realised that I had always been madly in love with you. From the beginning, from that first moment . . . something about you. It wasn't just physical attraction, although I pretended for a long while that it was. I felt stunned, as if I had been hit over the head . . . I found myself making mistakes, acting badly. I didn't feel in *control* any more. For a while getting right away seemed the only thing to do . . . I didn't know how to make you love me——'

'But I did!' Bethany smiled through her tears. 'When we made love on the beach . . . I knew, I really knew.' Bethany smiled in wonderment. 'We've always felt the same way about each other. We've always loved each other.'

'We'll burn the four-poster bed,' Chad announced, gazing down at her perceptively.

'No.' Bethany stroked a fingertip along the firm, sensuous mouth. 'There's no need for that. It's a beautiful bed. Our bed.'

Chad smiled and swept Bethany up into his arms, kissing her hungrily as he carried her slowly and surely across the hall, up the wide staircase and into the bedroom. Dark, sensuous eyes gazed down at her. 'Marry me, Bethany Jones?' he murmured huskily. 'I know you've been hurt before, but——'

She reached up a hand and touched Chad's lips, stilling his words with her fingers. 'You're right; the past doesn't matter any more,' she told him softly, 'only the future.'

'Is that a yes?' Chad queried urgently, pulling Bethany close against his hard, rugged length.

'Oh, darling, of course it is!' She smiled, her green eyes lingering lovingly on his face. 'You know I can't envisage my life without you ... When I found out you were going so far away——'

'Shh. Don't even think about it.' His mouth fell to her lips and he kissed her with a slow, lingering passion as he walked towards the bed and laid Bethany gently on to the rich golden covers.

'Show me how much you love me,' Bethany whispered. 'Please, Chad. Do it here. Do it now.'

He undressed her slowly, desire and love evident in every caress, in every kiss and touch.

Bethany's eyes misted over as they became one; she cried aloud as he finally brought her to the pinnacle of pleasure. But they were tears of joy and fulfilment, not sadness and pain.

Bethany smiled up into the strong, dark face, felt the pressure of Chad's firm, sensuous lips, and finally believed in fairy-tales.

Harlequin Romance®

Delightful

Affectionate

Romantic

Emotional

Tender

Original

Daring

Riveting

Enchanting

Adventurous

Moving

**Harlequin Romance—the
series that has it all!**

HROM-G

HARLEQUIN PRESENTS®

HARLEQUIN PRESENTS
men you won't be able to resist
falling in love with...

HARLEQUIN PRESENTS
women who have feelings
just like your own...

HARLEQUIN PRESENTS
powerful passion in
exotic international settings...

HARLEQUIN PRESENTS
intense, dramatic stories that will keep you
turning to the very last page...

HARLEQUIN PRESENTS
The world's bestselling romance series!

Harlequin® Historical

From rugged lawmen and
valiant knights to defiant heiresses
and spirited frontierswomen,
Harlequin Historicals will
capture your imagination with
their dramatic scope, passion
and adventure.

Harlequin Historicals...
they're too good to miss!